The Hunt of the Grimalkin

Dani Swanson

ISBN: 1533089779

ISBN-13: 978-1533089779

Cover design by Ana Ristovska

Edited by Erin Huber and Lisa Swanson

DEDICATION

To my loving family and friends who have put up with me with my passions. I appreciate the support and humor as I created.

Erin, thank you, for being my awesome editor and working through this process with me. Jessy, thank you, for helping me with the cover art. I couldn't have done it without you two!

To my loving boyfriend, Mike. Thank you for pushing me to be better and to chase after my art – both in paint and words.

CONTENTS

Chapter One

Laying in the soft grass, she could feel the sun slowly moving across her face, warming her skin and drying the light dew that covered her. She wanted to open her eyes but couldn't because of the searing pain in her head. She felt the fur of a little cat, nuzzling her hand that was lying on her stomach. Her lips parted to breathe deeper, and her chest rhythmically raised and lowered with each light breath, and a few soft sighs escaped.

She could feel every small rock and twig lost in the grass pressed against the skin on her legs as she ever so slowly started to stretch, still unable to open her eyes. She could feel her heartbeat from behind her eyes all the way to the back of her neck. Again, she felt the snuggling of a small purring cat, who meowed after each one of her sighs. She managed to open her eyes too small slits, allowing the bright rays of the sun to fill her sight. Rolling to her back, she moaned, louder and her head pounded harder the more she opened her eyes. After a few blinks, her green eyes were shining in the morning sun.

With a groan, she was able to pull herself up to her elbow and look at her surroundings but saw first the little orange cat that had been trying to rouse her. He sat on her stomach, observing her with his golden eyes fixed on her as if he was trying to convey a message. He meowed when he saw her eyes open. She raised a hand and started to scratch the cat behind his ear in an assumed guess at what he wanted. She slowly turned her head from left to right to survey the rest of her enviroment.

The trees were full of leaves and singing birds around the small lake. She could hear the babbling of a creek down the way. The grass was a thick carpet, and she could see the sun shining through the trees' branches. It was a beautiful, secluded area of a forest.

"Where am I?" she whispered to the cat.

She sat up, and the little cat jumped off her lap. She looked down and saw a plain, brown skirt bunched up to her knees and a pair of sandals lying not far from her feet. She had a few simple, metal rings on her fingers and a brown leather bag wrapped across her body. The more confused she became, the greater the pain in her head grew.

"What am I wearing?" again, she whispered. "What happened?" She searched desperately through the bag for a clue and found a few coins, a brush, an old key, and a note that read 'Make it home,' in a familiar scrawl. She rubbed her forehead as she continued to look around at the damp ferns, wide-eyed and confused.

"Where is home?" she questioned the little cat, whose eyes fixating behind her.

Stiffly and slowly with trepidation, she turned around to meet what the little cat was looking at. A bird hopped through the forest floor, its feathers shining a royal blue with a long neck and a tiny head. It pecked at the brush with its beak until it found a little grub and flew to the top of a nearby tree, right as the little cat pounced at the spot that the bird used to be. She then realized she didn't know where the little cat had come from. She had a blurry memory of a big, black tomcat.

She stood up and walked to the water's edge; the little cat followed her and lowered his head to drink. The water was still as a mirror in the sunshine and clear enough to see the smooth rocks on the bottom. She splashed some water on her face and stared at her reflection as the ripples calmed.

Her raven hair fell loosely about her round face. Her green eyes looked tired, with dark circles under them, as if she hadn't slept in some time.

She sat on the bank for a while, watching the cat and worried. Nothing felt familiar or right. She didn't recognize anything: where she was, what she was wearing, nor the little orange cat that had followed her. Nothing.

A grumble came from her stomach. "I guess I have to find something to eat," she said to the little cat. "You coming?"

"Meow."

The two started to walk west of the lake. She figured at least she could stay with the light and follow the sun. The forest was thick and had many different birds and creatures scampering in the shadows. She saw tiny tree frogs in shades of greens and reds jumping in the moss and birds of all colors singing in the trees. The little cat kept up with her pace through the trees as they followed a small brook runoff from the lake. A few small fish darted from bank to bank. Abruptly the little cat stopped, staring at the fish. He was in the water with a loud growl and small splash and had returned in a flash with a fish between his teeth. He dropped the flopping, finned creature at her feet, weaving in and out of her ankles, purring. Pleasantly surprised, she bent down and scratched his ears.

"Such a good boy! Now we need to figure out how to cook it." She looked around for a place to start a fire. She grabbed the wiggling fish, then grabbed a rock. "Sorry, fish," she muttered as she smashed its head.

She gathered some dry sticks and piled them next to her waiting meal. The little orange cat had settled next to the fish and would slyly lick it when she was not looking. She grabbed two rocks and hit them together to try to spark her kindling. She sat and pounded the stones over and over again. Her head was throbbing, and her stomach was in knots. She was exhausted and scared. Repeatedly she clicked the rocks on the dry wood. Little red sparks shot out, but none caught the brush. Tears started to roll down her cheeks; they felt hot as they made their way to her chin.

"Start," she whispered. "Start. Start. Why won't you start?" her voice got louder with each strike. She got mad and yelled, "Just start!" as she threw the rocks at the wood with a final clink of the stone. A small spark started to burn the brush. Her crying turned to laughter as she carefully blew on the ember. Soon she had a fire.

The little cat sat by the flames before he circled twice and laid down, purring in his sleep. She picked up a sharp-looking stick and pushed it through the fish, gagging the whole while. She roasted the fish over the fire as she rubbed her temple and watched the shadows dance on the forest floor around her. She ate the fish, ripping the pieces from the bones with her fingers, and fed some to her new feline friend.

"Do you have a name, little boy?" she asked the cat while he was cleaning his face after his dinner.

"Meow," he responded emphatically. His golden eyes seemed to smile at her as he continued to purr.

"Meow it is," she said with a smirk. She knew it was time to get going and at least find some shelter. Or, better yet, a person to ask where she was.

She stamped out the fire and went to have a drink from the brook. Meow followed her with a little sprint. They trailed the flowing water; Meow was splashing at fish, running ahead, and then waiting for her to catch up. There were flowers along the edge of the creek that swayed in the breeze. The sun was slowly starting to set, and it could have been a peaceful evening if she hadn't been so nervous about what would come with the darkness. Meow was no longer running ahead but was right next to her legs.

She was getting weak, tired, confused, and sore. Tears started to burn in the corner of her eyes for the second time since awakening in the woods. "Well, little cat, I'm not sure what to do anymore," she said, her voice cracking as she tried to hold back the tears. She sat down on a moss-covered rock, feeling defeated, and looked around.

She gave in and started to cry when suddenly all the little hairs on her arms stood up. She had the eerie feeling that someone was watching her. She stopped crying, held her breath in a gasp, and peered through the dense woods. She noticed that the little birds that had been singing could no longer be heard, no animals could be heard, and even the flowers seemed still like there was death in the air.

Slowly, she stood from where she sat and turned to inspect her surroundings, but nothing was there. Meow took the corner of her skirt in his mouth and started to tug. She looked down at him to see the cat's now puffed out his sleek tail on its ends. "You feel it too, don't you?" she whispered to him.

"Meow," he squeaked as he continued their trek down the brook. She cautiously followed behind the cat, always looking behind her. She saw a small branch that had fallen from one of the trees and decided to grab it. Perhaps it would be a good idea to carry a walking stick.

The peculiar silence slowly abated to the breeze's sounds and the birds, the farther down the creek they traveled. The water began to veer off to the left. When they reached the bend in the brook, Meow took off in a sprint straight ahead. "Hey!" she yelled after him, "Where are you going?!" She lifted her walking stick to her hip and ran after the cat in a panic. She already felt alone; there was no way she was going to let the one friend she had out of her sight. The trees were streaking past her in a blur of green. The forest thinned the farther they ran, trees becoming further spread apart.

Meow stopped unexpectedly at a break in the trees and sat nonchalantly licking his paws as she caught up to him. She huffed and gasped as she slowed to where the little orange cat waited. She could feel her heartbeat pounding in her temples and her chest. "Why?" she panted. "Why gasp did you gasp run gasp like that!?" Meow just rubbed against her leg and started to walk out of the woods.

The sun had started to set in the east now, and the sky was a watercolor painting of oranges and pinks that melted into dark blue. She could see the moon rising into the sky. She saw a rickety, thatched-roof cabin standing in the center of the clearing. The flowers and grass were overgrown around a broken stone wall that encircled the cabin. The small building was dark and looked as though it hadn't seen a visitor in some time. Meow, however, seemed to be comfortable there as if the place was familiar to him.

Cautiously, she walked towards the structure. What if there is someone there? She thought, becoming hopeful. What if they know where we are? Then she started to think of the feeling she had in the forest and was a little frightened. What if they are not friendly?

Chapter Two

She approached the run-down cabin and lightly rapped on the door. "Hello? Is someone in there?" she politely said in between knocks. "Hello?" The little building remained dark, and nothing was stirring inside. Meow scratched at the door as she was knocking.

"Meow," he said as he nudged the door with his head.

"Do you think I should try to go in?" she questioned out loud, encouraged by the cat's behavior. Her hand trembled as she reached for the latch. It was stiff as she turned it, but the door of the cabin was unlocked, and the door slowly creaked open as she pushed it with her finger tips. "Hello?" she said in a small voice as she stepped inside.

The inside was quaint; however, it was apparent that no one had visited this place in a long while. A thin layer of dust and cobwebs covered the furniture, and some sticks had fallen from the roof onto the stone floor. There were some candles on the table and a box of matches. She lit a few candles and then carried one around the room to see what she could find. There were various dishes and pots on the shelves around the fireplace, near an old pump sink. In one corner, a small bed with a little nightstand and a dresser created a sleeping area. There was a bookshelf by the door and a stuffed blue chair with dingy, gold buttons on the back. It was a nice little cabin that looked to be well cared for at one time.

The sun outside was almost gone below the trees and the warm temps left with the light. "I guess this is where we will be for the night," she said to the little orange cat. His eyes glowed in the candlelight as he started to purr. She couldn't help but wonder why a small cabin was here in the middle of nowhere and why someone would just leave all of their stuff here.

She found a small stack of wood by the fireplace and started a fire, which lit the little cabin's walls. She drew the curtains over a couple of narrow windows. She noticed she had left the door open and that her little furry friend was gone. She immediately felt anxious, as the only interaction she had was with that cat, and now he was nowhere to be seen. She went out on the porch and noticed that the curtains blocked the bright light of the fireplace. She peered out into the darkness. The chill of the night air blew across her face as her gaze raked the forest edge. As the wind blew, a shiver ran down her spine, and she lightly shuddered as she wrapped her arms around her waist for warmth.

All at once, the sounds of her surroundings were muted – no rustle of the wind, no crickets. She felt sad and alone. She started to turn towards the door to go back in when she saw two yellow eyes glowing in the dark, moving towards her rapidly. The large shadowy figure was mammoth and flowing as if gliding through the air. She gasped, spun on her heels into the cabin, slamming the door shut behind her.

She sat against the door, holding the latch as she held her breath, trying not to make a sound. What is happening? She thought as she felt her heartbeat harder and harder in her chest. She jumped when she heard a light scratching on the door. She sat there for a moment and started to breathe again. Scratch. Scratch. Scratch. She swallowed hard; her shoulders shook with fear. The room seemed to be getting darker, and she held her breath again.

Scratch.

Scratch.

Scratch.

"Meow?" came the sweet sound from the other side of the door. She let out a slow breath. The room started to come back into focus. She stood and opened the door slowly to see the adorable little orange cat with a bigger fish than his own body. Meow had gone to catch the dinner. She stuck her head out of the door and looked into the darkness. There was no sign of the giant creature she had seen running through the dark. The breeze was back to rustling everything outside, and the crickets were chirping in the night.

There they sat in the overstuffed blue chair with the dingy gold buttons. Her feet were kicked up on a small ottoman, and the little orange cat sat on her lap purring while they waited for the fish to cook. The cabin's dusty smell was airing out, and the smell of boiled fish filled the room. She felt comfortable here. Sitting in the cozy chair with the little cat on her lap felt familiar; however, she could not remember anything clearly. She rubbed her temple, trying to get rid of the fog in her head as she scratched behind Meow's ear.

She found some blankets in a trunk at the foot of the bed that were not covered in dust and made up the little bed for the night. With the blankets wrapped around her, she sank into the soft billows of the bed. She cuddled up, trying to fight the cool dampness coming in through the few unpatched areas of the roof. She couldn't get her brain to calm down; it was racing over all the unknowns she had experienced throughout the day. The frustrations of not knowing how she got there, of not being able to remember anything leading up to her waking up by the lake. Everything felt so familiar, yet so strange all in the same moment.

Softly sighing, she slowly fell asleep. Her dreams were snapshots of bright lights and people whose faces she couldn't make out. Shadowy figures were dancing around a fire, shooting stars flashing past their heads, laughter, and giddy shrieks. Then nothing but cold, dark, wetness.

Boom! She awoke to the crashing of thunder. Lightning

danced on the dark walls—rain dripping through the roof, landing in small pots that had been left there from before. Meow was curled at her side, licking her hand to comfort her. She laid her head back down onto the pillow and gently stroked the cat's head. "I thought this was part of the dream," she whispered.

The rain hadn't let up by morning, though it was a little brighter in the cabin. She added more wood to the fireplace embers and snacked on the leftover boiled fish with her furry friend. She placed a small dish of water on the floor for Meow so he wouldn't have to go outside. Her curiosity about the house got the better of her, and she started to dig through everything she could find as she slowly cleaned away the built-up dust.

"What do you think we might find, Meow? Treasures? Clues? I wish you could talk back to me," she chimed to the cat.

"Meow," he responded as he settled on the ottoman, washing his face. She wiped down the tables and washed the dishes. She dusted around the fireplace and found a small knife that she put in her bag. It had a carved wooden handle with a little leather sheath covering the blade.

"I don't think anyone will miss it," she said with a shrug. She dug through the trunk and found a pair of pants made of a dark canvas about her size. A small pantry behind the fireplace held some dried goods: flour, sugar, hay, and spices. There were some more books and clothes in the back as well. She used some of the grass to patch the leaky parts of the roof as best she could.

She sat down in the overstuffed blue chair with Meow and looked through the bookshelf. There was a small wooden box that chimed a song when she opened it. The pain in her head started to throb with the tones. She closed her eyes and hummed the tune. "I know this song," she said slowly to

Meow. Meow, however, showed no interest in what was happening and settled in for a nap. Inside the box, a beautiful pendant had the most transparent red stone she had ever seen. It hung on a glistening silver chain with scrolling details holding the stone in place. It was breathtaking. "Why would someone leave this behind?" She questioned as the music box started the song over. She shut the box with the pendant back inside of it. *Someone will be back for that,* she thought to herself. *They would have to be.*

She pulled out one of the books and started to read the story of a girl who fell in love with a prince. About three-quarters of the way through the book, she found a small piece of paper used as a bookmark. She stared at it in disbelief. The paper said: 'Fig knows the way.' She jumped up from where she sat; Meow went flying in the air in a big puff of orange fur and a hiss. "Sorry, kitty," she said as she raced for her bag. The scrap she found in the book was the same size, color, and texture as the note she had in her bag. The paper had the same old musty smell and the color of the ink matched.

Most importantly, the rough edges of both papers fit perfectly together. 'Make it home. Fig knows the way.'

"Who is Fig?!" she yelled.

"Meow."

Her little orange companion, who was sitting on the edge of the overstuffed chair, had stopped smoothing out his fur and was watching her pace about the room. His golden eyes were wide, and his ears pushed forward. She continued to pace back and forth in the room, talking out loud. "How am I supposed to make it home when I don't know where home is? Who is this Fig? What the hell does this mean?!" she yelled.

"Meow," the cat again said and looked at her with wide eyes.

She stopped pacing.

"Fig?" she whispered, and the cat responded with another meow. "Fig. Your name is Fig?" The cat meowed again and walked over to her, and rubbed against her legs. "Well, if you're Fig, did you just bring me home?

Chapter Three

She sat on the floor, slowly rocking back and forth with a fixation on the two pieces of paper. Fig sat and watched her with his head tilted to one side. With her pointer fingers pressed to her lips, she swayed, puzzling out the new evidence.

"Did I leave myself clues? Or did someone leave me these?" she mumbled. Fig walked over to her and brushed up on her side, then walked over to the storage room's door and pawed it.

She slowly stood up and put the little pieces of paper into her pocket. She walked over to the pantry and started to move everything out into the main space. There were small wooden boxes, ribbons, clothes, books, and tools. She brought each thing out and dug through them, searching for another little paper to add to the two she had collected.

"Fig, I am not seeing a reason you want me to dig in this closet."

She found a bag that had peppermint, lavender, honey, cinnamon, ginger, and other herbs. Deeper and deeper into the crowded closet, she went. She froze when she got to the back. Under an old sheet in the very back corner was a painting. She stared into the bright green eyes of a round-faced girl with raven hair. She was looking into her own eyes in a portrait of which she had no memories. She brought it out to the main room, into the light, and studied the painting. It was her. Her head was tilted to the side, and her eyes smiled more than her lips. She had a ribbon tied into her hair, and the bright red pendant she had found in the box was around her neck. She massaged her temple and watched Fig rub his scent on the picture and purr. She listened to the rain falling outside and looked around the room. "Am I home?"

She hung the painting above the mantle and started to organize the items that she found. She had books on medicine and stories of far-off lands, none of which revealed any more hidden messages as bookmarks. She filled her bookshelf with her finds and decided to put on the necklace she had found before. As she took it out of the music box, she felt an icy surge run through her as the cool stone touched her bare skin. She boiled some water over the fire and added the lavender to it; the scent filled the entire cabin with the sweet, sleepy smell. She took some of her concoction and applied it to her temple.

She didn't know why she needed to do this, but it seemed instinctual. For a little while, the pain went away, and she got sleepy from the scent of the lavender. She changed into the clothes that she had found in the pantry. She snacked on some odds and ends that she had found on the shelves. Little Fig went out in the rain and came back licking his chops; it appeared he had taken care of his dinner for the night.

The cabin was clean and organized. She plopped down on the overstuffed blue chair with the dingy, gold buttons and started to read one of the medicinal books she had found. It showed how to heal colds with honey and upset stomachs with peppermint. The book was all handwritten, by different hands and inks. Some had drawings of the plants to use and how to prepare them. "Interesting," she murmured. Fig lazily lifted his head before rolling onto his other side to sleep.

They snuggled up on the chair, and she flipped through books. She found one that piqued her curiosity. The book was leather-bound with gold lettering that read 'Creatures.' "Even more interesting, Fig." The little cat purred as she read through all the different creatures she found on the pages.

'The Epimelides are beautiful tree nymphs with hair the color of apple blossoms and soft as undyed sheep's wool. They protect apple trees and sheep. They can change the shapes between trees and humans. They like to play tricks on humans for fun.'

Next to the description was a beautiful coal drawing of a little tree with a woman's face. "Have you ever seen one of those, Fig?" She showed the picture to the sleepy kitty. He viewed the image with wide eyes and meowed at her. He pawed at the book and knocked it to the floor. "Hey!" she playfully yelled at the cat as she bent down to pick up the book. The pages had fallen open to show a large, shadowy, cat-shaped creature on it.

The subtitle labeled it, 'Grimalkin.' Curiously, she read on, "An all-black, cat-like shadow creature with bright green eyes and a white spot on its chest. The grimalkin travels at night, stealing the souls of those it captures. It has been said that a witch's cackle can be heard shortly before the large cat appears." As she settled back into her chair with her little furry friend, she started to creep herself out with every fairy, nymph, dragon, or monster she read about in the book of creatures.

After a time, she put the book down and looked around the little cabin. The rain still rhythmically fell onto the roof, and the fire had finally warmed the walls of the tiny abode. She let out a sigh of contentment, enjoying the warmth, cleanliness, and sweet smell of lavender. She finally felt a sense of comfort. The pain in her head, though still there, had dulled. Despite the comfort, things did not yet make any sense. She twisted the pendant between her fingers, and it cooled her fingers. She didn't know what to think. At this point, she was just starting to accept that she was where she was supposed to be, even if she could not remember anything before two days ago.

She curled up in bed with Fig in the nook of her arm, purring as he softly snored a little cat snore. Tonight she drifted off into a dreamless sleep.

Scratch.

Scratch.

Scratch.

She stirred in her sleep.

Scratch.

She slowly opened her eyes as she stretched her arms over her head. She looked down and saw Fig standing erect, staring at the door. The cat's puffed his tail with hairs on end, and his ears were pinned back. A low throaty growl was coming from his throat. Scratch. Scratch. Noises came from the other side of the door, then from under the window, and then back at the door. She reached for her bag and got out the little knife. She slowly got to her feet and crept to the window. She pulled back the corner of the curtain and peered into the darkness. Fig let out a cry that sounded like nothing she had ever heard before. It sounded like a war cry that a lion would roar. She dropped the curtain just as a shadowy figure started to run toward the forest. When the lightning struck and lit up the field, she could see the large black model reach the edge of the trees; just as quickly as it appeared, it vanished into nothing.

She was trembling as she looked out into the grim nothingness. Fig's tail had returned to average size, and his ears were no longer pinned to his head. She sat on the edge of the bed and stared at the window uneasily. Fig came and nudged her arm as if he was trying to comfort her. They laid back down on the soft bed. Sleep did not come back, at least not soundly. When the morning came, the sun came too. The rain had finally stopped, and the warm daylight filled the windows of the cabin.

They ventured outside onto the rickety porch. Everything had a light dew covering it that glistened in the sun. There was a small vegetable garden off to the side that she hadn't noticed that first night. It had become overgrown and ravaged by many critters. There was nothing around the clearing except for trees in all directions.

She went back inside and picked up a few of the books, the bag of herbs, the knife, and the matches. She changed into the pants she had found and tied a cloak over her shoulders. "Fig, I have to find people. I need to know where I am. Who I am." The cat looked as if he understood and walked to the door, waiting for her to open it.

Fig dashed out to the left. Naturally, she followed the cat. After all, Fig knows the way.

Chapter Four

Walking through the woods, collecting nuts and berries along the way, she hummed the song from the music box. She often stopped looking through her book of herbs, roots, and berries and collected the ones that weren't poisonous. She didn't want to go without food again. Little Fig ran through the forest and had a rodent for lunch as she munched on berries and brassica root. The path they were on continued West. Soon the trees started to thin, and it became more of a road beneath their feet instead of the mossy way they had started on. Following the sun down the trail, she saw something over the tops of the trees. Smoke. Swirling grey billows of smoke were dancing above the trees as they came out of a chimney stack in the distance. "Look, Fig!" she squealed with excitement. The little tabby looked up at her and meowed.

The smoke was still far off in the distance, but it gave her hope. As they walked on, she started to get that same feeling that they were not alone. Hairs on the back of her neck standing on end as she looked down at Fig. He had stopped moving and was staring behind her with his tail puffed out, and his ears pinned back. Slowly she turned around and looked in the direction of the cat's glare. She saw a large shadow darting away from them through the trees. She spoke through a lump in her throat as she yelled after it, "What do you want? I see you!" She scooped up a rock and threw it in the direction where the shadow figure had been. A cackling laugh echoed through the trees and diminished. Fig hissed.

"What was that," she panted. Could a grimalkin be a real thing?

She bent down and started petting Fig until his tail returned to its normal size. They began to walk again, but she always looked back over her shoulder.

As she continued to walk down the road, she noticed a sweet

smell drifting through the air. "Cinnamon?" she deduced. "Do you smell that, Fig?" The scent was filling her nose as they walked, but where could it be coming from? The billowy smoke was still a few miles ahead, and all she could see were trees and the forest floor glowing in the sunshine.

Fig turned his head to the side as if listening intently to something. He crouched down and began to stalk some unseen prey, ready to pounce. He crept ever so slowly towards a small boulder covered in moss. "What are you doing, cat? We need to keep going," she followed after him, attempting to scoop him up, but he was too quick for her grasp. He moved to the bottom of the rock toward a group of mushrooms. The smell of cinnamon grew stronger as she followed Fig. "What is that?" she asked with a whisper. She tilted her head to one side, and a curious smile spread across her lips. "What is it?" she whispered again.

The little mushroom cluster had a glowing light that wasn't from the sunshine. The mushrooms were all in a circle, and the strange light seemed to come from the fungi themselves. She laid down on her stomach in the soft mossy grass and put her face down by the mushrooms. Fig perched himself on top of the boulder, staring down at the mushrooms like a vulture. She couldn't believe what she was seeing. There were windows in the mushrooms! Tiny, little windows with a golden light pouring through the panes. She could see shadows moving around behind those panes. She pulled her book of creatures out of her bag, flipping to a charcoal drawing in the back that had a picture of mushrooms in the same shape. 'Fairy Circle' was written underneath it. She smiled. "Fairies?" she whispered.

When she spoke, all the movement inside the tiny house stopped. The lights went out. "Sorry. I don't mean any harm," she whispered as she slowly crept away from the circle. She got to her feet and picked Fig up as she slowly walked away.

As she turned to go, there was a whirlwind of color swirling around her head. Her long raven hair was getting pulled every which way and over her eyes, covering her line of sight. She felt short, sharp pains in her arms and legs. Her eyes got heavy, and she fell with a large thump. Right before she shut her eyes, she saw a woman wearing green leaves with hot pink hair. She had a saber in her hand, and silvery wings were fluttering furiously. The fairy was no bigger than her index finger.

When she woke up, her head was throbbing again, with a fuzzy feeling lingering in the front of her eyes. She was lying on the side of the road, with Fig asleep on her stomach. She grabbed the side of her head and winced as the trees swirled around her in a drunken stupor. "Oh, my head!" she whined. Fig woke up and shook his head. He seemed cross-eyed. The sun had set, and it had become cold. She sat up and brushed the dirt off of her arms as Fig washed his face. She pulled out her creature book and flipped through it to the section where the fairies were listed. She read about how they were territorial, their use of a mixture of wild lettuce and passion flowers brewed with cinnamon to subdue their enemies. She couldn't believe what she had seen or what had happened.

She started to shiver in the cold night's air. She moved in farther into the woods and leaned her back up against a tree. She was too afraid to start a fire, she didn't want to alert anyone or anything that she was there, but it was too dark for them to see the dirt road anymore. She wrapped the cloak around her shoulders and cuddled up with Fig. She didn't bother closing her eyes, knowing sleep would evade her, and jumped at every sound she heard.

Deeper in the woods, she saw the lights of the fairy circle come to life again. She watched from where she sat; she didn't dare to go any closer and rubbed her head as she thought about the confusing experience. Unbeknownst to her, the tiny fairy with the hot pink hair was fluttering far above her in the tree, watching her watch the fairy circle.

Fig had also been on guard all night, never leaving her side. As dawn brightened, she could see a little more clearly, and she surveyed the woods. She realized that some of the birds that she saw flying through the forest weren't birds at all. They were little fairies soaring back and forth between the trees, racing from branch to branch.

She pulled her book out of her bag and started to study all the creatures in the book. 'How can this be real?' she thought to herself in awe. Her head throbbed. Her side was sore from her fall. Her stomach growled; the berries just weren't cutting it anymore. She rested her head on the tree and watched the little fairies swoop about with the birds. They gracefully danced amongst the vines and trees. One tiny fairy caught her eye; he glowed with a green hue and didn't fly as fast as the others did. He bobbed more than fluttered. He was slowly looping down, headed towards the fairy circle, when all of a sudden, he dropped hard, straight to the ground.

She immediately jumped up and ran to where the green orb had fallen; there he laid in a slump, not moving. She gingerly picked him up and rested him in her hand. She intuitively started to rub his stomach with her pointer finger. "Please wake up, little guy, please?" she whispered to him. She felt a surge of electricity run through her veins and out her finger, connecting her with the fairy. The hair on her head whirled around her. For a brief moment, the pain in her head subsided.

The other little fairies congregated around her as she sat with the little fairy. The green aura that had surrounded the fairy was now encompassing them both. Her raven hair blew away from her face as if a fierce wind was blowing on her. She could hear the chattering from the fairies, but all she could see was the green light. She started to feel light-headed and sick to her stomach. The green light began to spin in circles around them. Faster and faster until the electricity between her hand and the little fairy stopped. It ended just as suddenly as it had started. Her hair fell limp around her face, and the small faces of hundreds of fairies and one orange cat came into focus. She slumped over to her side with labored breaths. The little green fairy, still safely in her hand, lifted his head from her palm and turned to face her. "Thank you," his small voice squeaked before he flew into the crowd.

"She… saved him," the little pink-haired fairy stammered.

She felt tired, worn out, and sick. Her stomach was growling, but the thought of food made her nauseous. Her head was pounding again behind her right eye. She struggled to concentrate on anything going on around her. It felt like a confusing dream, and yet, like Deja Vu as well.

The fairies had brought her to the center of their home in the forest. She noticed how the fairy homes seemed to be formed in concentric circles, becoming less crowded and grander the closer to the center they went. They brought her some dried meat, cheese, and fruit to eat and a bottle of wine. They settled in the center of the large fairy circle; more and more fairies came out to see her. The elaborate homes were no longer just mushrooms but entire trees, and she could see the golden light shining out from their windows through the bark and the mushrooms. She sat with the pink-haired fairy and watched the other busy fairies dance and play.

"How did you do it? Where are you from? Where are you going? Why are you here? What is your name?" The fairy was talking a mile a minute in her ear. "What is your name?" The fairy asked her. "They call me Willow," she offered in her small voice without waiting for a response. Willow then continued to ask variations of the same question over and over again, "How did you do that?"

"I have no idea how I did that," the girl finally answered in a confused voice.

"And I was going west to try to find someone to tell me where I am." Willow sat down on her knee to listen to her answers. Fig, on her other side, nervously watched Willow. "And I'm from… well my name is..." she started to panic. She still couldn't remember anything from before waking up a few days ago on the bank of the river. "I'm sorry," she said with a lump in her throat, choking back tears. "I can't seem to remember who I am or where I came from." Crocodile tears poured from her eyes and rolled down her cheeks. Willow watched her with a look of concern on her face.

The distraught girl continued to tell her story to the small fairy through her tears. She recounted how she woke up, met Fig, and followed him through the forest. She told Willow about the cabin in the middle of the woods and the strange shadow she had seen a couple of times. She displayed her book, 'Creatures,' and the scraps of paper with her handwritten clues. She got so upset telling her story she started to hyperventilate.

Willow flew up from her spot and got close to her face. She could see little gold specs shining on Willow's face, and her blue eyes stared back into hers. "You need to breathe!" she squeaked in a panic as she squeezed the girl's cheeks. The girl shut her eyes and started to slow her breathing between hiccups.

"What am I going to do?" the girl sobbed. Willow had confronted her with the questions that had been plaguing her befuddled mind, and it was overwhelming.

Willow and the other fairies made a blanket for the girl out of all their blankets, an incredible masterpiece in its own right. Hundreds of blankets stitched together in a patchwork of color and materials: leather, feathers, moss, wool, and a slippery substance she couldn't name. The girl covered as much of herself with it as she could and stared blankly into the fire. Fig sat at her feet, carefully watching the fairies and the girl with a look of concern. His tail had not gone down the entire time he was in the fairy circle. The girl rested her chin on her folded arms upon her knees, slowly rocking herself as one would comfort a crying baby.

"You'll find the way. You'll remember," Willow said, trying to be comforting. The little green fairy whom she had saved flew up to her, pressed a tender kiss on her forehead, and dropped a vile in her lap before passing away. The container shimmered in the moonlight with millions of specks of silver. "Fairy dust," Willow explained. "You can use it for your magic."

The girl started to cry again; then, her tears turned to hysterical laughter as she laid her head back. Most of the fairies were frightened by her abrupt laugh and scattered to their houses. Willow stayed and looked at her. "You have magic. You may not remember it, but you used it today."

"All I did was pick up a fairy and hold him," the girl responded, with a cynical tone to her voice. "I haven't done anything but wander uselessly for days."

Willow flew up and condescendingly patted the girl on her cheek. It wasn't very reassuring.

The fire slowly burned down; the little fairies that were still up watching the girl from afar retired to their homes. Fig curled up on the girl's cloak and slept softly. Willow stayed up with the girl and mirrored how she was sitting watching the fire, except she was facing the girl, seated on the girl's forearm. A few crickets chirping in the distance and the crackling of the embers were all that could be heard. "Let me see your book," Willow said after a long silence.

The girl started at the little voice. She reached over to her bag and pulled out the old leather book. She set the book down, and the little fairy hovered over the words to read about all the creatures it stored. Willow would occasionally talk aloud to herself with a, "Yes, that's right," or would say something was incorrect.

The girl slowly started to shake her pensive mood and paid attention to the fairy. She was awestruck as the fairy flipped the pages by merely guiding her hand over a page. "You need to fix this page. The unicorns cannot fly, and they eat grass just like a regular horse," Willow said. The girl pulled a pencil out of her bag, writing in the margins of the book of creatures. She didn't know if any of it would be relevant to her, but it was distracting her from the sick feeling still running through her body.

"Grimalkin," Willow's voice trailed off as she read the page.

"I think I have seen that thing. I think it is following us." The girl said to Willow.

Willow turned her head slowly with a fearful look on her face. "Did you see the witch, or did you see the shadow?" the fairy asked.

"The shadow. It looked like a huge lion with glowing eyes." Willow stared out into the darkness and said in a tiny voice. "Be careful of traveling through the forest in the dark. She likes to jump on people's backs from behind and steal their souls. Then you see people and creatures wandering around the forest with a stupefied look on their faces. I don't know where they end up going, but they look like they are dead. You should get a weapon. Something sharp." Willow trailed off as she continued to read the book.

Willow and the Girl stayed up throughout the night and discussed gnomes, shadows, nymphs, and dragons. "Tell me. How many fairies are there here?" The girl asked.

"Well, in this kingdom, there are 7,365 fairies. There are seven other kingdoms that I know about in the forest. But I haven't made it to all corners of the forest yet, so there may be more. Each kingdom has a royal family that rules over a part of the forest." Willow stated.

"Oh? Where is the castle?" the girl asked.

Willow started to laugh at her. "We don't live in castles, you silly human. We live in the trees and the mushrooms." Willow giggled.

"Oh." The girl said sheepishly.

"They live in that old oak tree." The fairy pointed to the outskirts of the fairy circle to a giant tree in the area. The girl could see a faint golden light coming from the top of the tree. "They have been watching you since you got here," Willow whispered conspiratorially to her with a smile. "Anastasia, the fairy queen, and her children live there. She is the fairest fairy you will ever lay eyes on. She has golden hair that shines as bright as the sun, and her glow is the lightest pink shimmer I've ever seen." Willow was in awe of the queen. "Her poor husband fell in the last battle against the Starling Kingdom. They attacked our kingdom to try to take our territory away from the lake. The water nymphs had gnomes attacking our houses while we slept. The rest of the fairy warriors went out and attacked their kingdom too. We lost a lot of fairies." She said sadly.

"Is the Starling Kingdom another group of fairies?" the girl asked.

"Yes," Willow answered. "We are the Sparrow Kingdom." She said, pointing to her green sword. The girl held it close to her face and was able to see a small sparrow engraved into the handle. "That was many years ago, but the queen doesn't leave her home very often. She watches from her window and sends sparrows down with her messages." She was very solemn in her delivery. They sat in silence for a while and watched the fire burning low in the pit. "Well, it's late. You should try to rest. You still aren't looking well." Willow excused herself and fluttered to a little mushroom near the edge of the fairy circle. The girl curled up on her bed of moss and covered herself up with her blanket from the fairies and her cloak. Fig nuzzled into her arm and purred softly.

Chapter Five

The girl awoke to chokecherries and explosions falling around. Willow zoomed by her face and yelling, "Girl! Human! Get up! We're being attacked!"

The girl looked up to see Fig jumping up in the air and attacking tree elves riding on the back of ravens; the elves were bombing the circle. The elves were not much bigger than the fairies. They were all dressed in brown with little green hats. They had the darkest black hair and pointed ears spilling out from under their hats. Their emerald eyes looked angry as they swooped in.

The girl jumped up and started to swat at the birds flying around her head. She picked up a branch from the fire pit that had not burned all the way through and swung at the birds and elves flying through the air. Sparks flew when the elves and fairies collided. Pink, green, red, and blue orbs spun around the fairy circle. Ravens were falling from the sky and scooping up fallen elves. Once the girl had started in the battle, the majority of the birds flew away in fright.

There was a rainbow of colored orbs scattered on the ground. Many of the fairies were not moving. She sat down panting against a rock and rested in the moss. "Can you help them?" A breathless Willow spatters out in her tiny voice.

The girl looked up to see the warrior fairies bringing their injured over to the girl. "I…I don't know what to do! I told you that yesterday!" She cried.

"You can do it again! You have to!" Willow yelled in a panic.
"I... I'll try," she stuttered.

The girl placed her pointer finger on the bellies of a fallen fairy and rubbed it back and forth. The electric current she had felt the day before came over her once again. Running through her body and out her fingertips, the little fairy started to levitate in the air. Her raven hair extended off her head and swayed in the air. She shut her eyes tight and held her breath until the current stop running through her finger. One after another, she had the fairies until they were all up flying around the circle.

When the last fairy was brought over to the girl, she could see that the little fairy wasn't breathing. The girl laid the fairy in her hand as she had done for all the rest of them. She rubbed the little fairy's tummy just as before. Nothing happened. "I'm sorry, I think she is gone," the girl said in a weak voice to Willow. "It's not working," the girl continued to try for what felt like forever before Willow told her to stop.

The girl felt exhausted and then saw something dark move in the long grass. A little elf was stirring on the ground who had been left behind. He was disorientated and bleeding. The girl reached over to the long grass and grabbed the little elf. "I've got you," she whispered to him.

"What do you think you are doing?!" a little blue fairy yelled at the girl.

"They attacked us!" Willow hissed at the girl.

She looked at the fairies and said, "I can't let him die," in a stern voice. As she had done to the fairies, she did the same to the elf. The current ran through her body and put her finger to his body. This time she left her eyes open and watched as the cut on the little elf's head slowly started to reverse itself until the head was completely healed. Just as it started, the current stopped. The elf lifted his head and opened his eyes wide with fright. He looked around the circle and saw the human holding him. He drew his dagger and dug it deep into the girl's hand before running off into the trees.

"See?" the blue fairy yelled at the girl. "They're evil!"

The girl pulled the dagger out of her palm, which had to be no bigger than a splinter. She slowly started to rise from her spot. "I feel strange..." she said as she tried to stand. The girl's eyes rolled back into her head before she made it all the way to her feet, and she fell over into a slump. The fairies flew around her in a flutter. Their voices merged into a sound of static. Fairy dust was flying wildly through the air. Fig ran over to the girl and licked her hand, and nudged her. The girl did not move but sighed in her sleep.

"She's moving!" a small voice yelled.

The girl opened her eyes to see hundreds of small faces watching her from the shadows. She saw they brought her into a leaf-covered space under a giant shrub, where they had hollowed out the inside to cover her from the elements. The blanket that the fairies had made her was tucked around her, and Fig was licking her face.

"What happened?" she rubbed her head and sat up as much as she could under the branches.

"You've been asleep for four days," Willow said to her.

The girl sat up and coughed up black bile onto the dirt floor. She gingerly climbed out of the shrub, dragging the blanket with her. After some food and water, she was able to get up to her feet. She stumbled a little with her first few steps but then was able to move around. "Willow, I think it's time I go and find a real bed to sleep in," the girl announced.

"We made you something!" a small male voice came from behind her. The little green fairy that she had saved initially was watching her with large eyes.

"Well, give it to her, Pix," Willow said. Pix showed the girl her cloak that she had worn, only now it was sparkling with silver glitter and a symbol of a sparrow on the back of it. She smiled at the little fairies and thanked them for the gift. "Be careful," Willow said to the girl. "Stay away from those elves; we told you they were evil."

She looked down at her hand, at the little scratch she still had from where the elf had stabbed her. She wondered if the elf did poison her or if her reaction was to her magic.

As she packed her things, Willow came up and stood on the girl's shoulder. "Are you sure you want to leave?" she asked the girl.

"I'm too big here. I can't just sit in one spot all the time. Besides, I still don't know who I am or how I got here. I need to find someone who knows," the girl responded. Willow sat down on the girl's shoulder.

"I know who you are," Willow said in her ear.

"Who?!" the girl yelled. Willow covered her ears and balled up in pain, almost falling off the girl's shoulder. The girl picked Willow up by her shoulder and held her in her palm. She held Willow near her face and spoke softly and slowly to the little fairy. "If you know who I am, you need to tell me." Willow cautiously took her hands away from her ears and looked up at the girl with big eyes.

"Well, I meant, I know who you are now. We named you." The girl looked down in shock, feeling both flattered and disgusted that they named her. "You named me....like a pet?" she accused.

"No!" the fairy insisted. "Everyone needs to be called

something. We can't just call you girl or human. We started to call you Cannenta. It means a woman with the power to heal," Willow said to her sheepishly.

She smiled appeased. "Thank you, Willow, that's very sweet."

The fairies filled her bag full of meat, cheese, and other foods. They folded up their quilted blanket and tied it in a bundle for her to attach to her bag. She put on her cloak with the silver sparrow and said her good-byes as she started back towards the main path again. She was leaving with more questions than she had answers. The more she tried to remember, the more her head hurt. Fig trotted behind her. He seemed happy to be away from the fairy circle.

They walked down the path towards where they saw the smoke. The day got warmer as the sun rose higher in the sky. The trees started to thin the farther they walked. They stopped for lunch at the edge of the trees that opened to a large pasture. A few deer cautiously walked through the long grass, and some wild horses playing in the sun.

She saw what appeared to be a small farm, or at least what was left of one. The buildings all had peeling paint and faded shutters. The fences were broken down in some places, which seemed fine since there were no animals around. Someone lived there, though; she could see the light grey smoke spiral up into the sky. "What do you think, Fig?" she asked the orange cat. He sat on the edge of a log and had his head tilted to the side. He was eating a bit of pickled fish that Willow had sent with them.

"Meow," He answered as he licked his paw and then rubbed his chubby cheeks.

"Oh, you think so?" she said jokingly. "I guess we'd better go check it out."

Before they started, she pulled a brush out of her bag, ran it through her hair, and checked her face in her small hand mirror. She wanted to make sure she was presentable for whomever she was to meet. She had lost track of how many days she'd been gone from the cabin but felt that it was starting to show in her appearance. She wanted to sleep in a bed.

They walked across the field; Fig was playing with a couple of toads, hopping through the grass while watching her step not to twist her ankle on a rock. As they neared the broken-down fence, she could smell bread baking. The gate opened with a loud squeak and then crashed shut with a bang. "Well, we won't be sneaking up on them," she said in a whisper. She walked up to the run-down little farmhouse and, with a deep breath and knocked on the door three times. She could hear movement inside.

A deep voice from inside replied, "Just a minute!" A few moments later, she heard the bolt being released on the door and out poked the nose of a little old man. He barely came up to her ribs in height and had a long, grizzly beard that dragged on the floor. He had kind eyes that smiled behind his little square glasses. He grinned and showed his gapped-tooth mouth to her. "Why hello there! I haven't seen you in ages!" he chirped.

She felt a surge of relief take over her body. The pounding in her chest had subsided. "You remember who I am?!" she exclaimed to the little man.

He looked startled at her excitement. "I was talking to him," he said in his deep voice, gesturing to Fig.

"Meow," said the little cat as he rubbed upon the man's legs in a greeting. Fig walked past the man's legs and plopped down at the fire.

"Now, who are you, miss?" he directed back to the girl. She felt her face turning red as she looked back at the little man. "That's an excellent question," she replied.

After some time, the little man listened to her story and finally invited her into the house. He fixed her a plate of homemade bread and some cheese. She offered him some of the dried meat that she had gotten from Willow. She learned that his name was Flynn, and he had lived there at the farm his entire life. As the girl took a bite of the bread, she remembered the sweet taste of cardamom dancing on her tongue. The pain in her head started to throb again as she attempted to evoke the memories attached to the taste.

"I do recognize you," Flynn said between bites. "You go to the market on Tuesdays. I remember you saved that guy who fell off his horse. He was hurt pretty bad, but you gave him something out of your bag there, and he walked away as if nothing had happened. That was the last time I remember seeing you. I think that was a few months ago," he said to her. "But this little guy still goes to the market on Tuesdays, even though you haven't been there." He scratched under the sleepy kitty's chin. Fig opened his eyes when Flynn stopped scratching him and meowed as if in protest.

"Can you tell me anything else about me?" she asked Flynn in a small unsure voice. He rocked back and forth on the back legs of his chair while he nibbled on a little piece of bread. "Well, I know that you have sold a lot of different things in the market. You have a stall there. You sell medicine and art stuff for people's houses. I saw you weaving a blanket one time with my wife, Eleonore. She should be back in the morning if you want to meet her. Maybe she knows more about you. I just know that you buy my bread each week."

She smiled big at Flynn, with the potential of meeting someone who knows who she could be.

"If you come back tomorrow, I'm sure she would love to talk to you." He finished his thought and planted the chair back on the ground.

"Oh," she murmured disappointedly. "It took me a few days to get here. I'm not sure if I'll make it back. I'm not sure where I'm going or how to get back to where I came from. I had better find someplace to go for the evening. Thank you for your hospitality," She said as she slowly stood up from the stool. "Which way is the market?" she questioned him.

"If you don't have anywhere to stay, you are more than welcome to stay out in the barn. I couldn't explain having a young girl sleeping in my house to the wife." He grabbed his little walking stick and wobbled over to the closet door, and removed a pillow and a blanket from the shelves. "Come on then." He said in his gruff voice as they walked out the back of the house. "It's not much, but it will keep the chill off of you."

The barn, with red peeling paint, had a loft full of hay. There were no animals in the barn, but the stalls looked as if they were prepared for critters to live in them. "We'll see you in the morning," Flynn said as he turned to leave. "Keep the door latched," she heard him warn as he hobbled back up to the house.

The Girl and Fig curled up upon a haystack with the fairy blanket and the blanket the little old man gave her and settled in for the night. "Well, this is better than sleeping outside," she said to Fig as she adjusted the hay not to stick her through the blanket.

The wind was howling outside. She could see the clouds around the moon through the cracked window of the barn; they glided eerily across the crescent. She drifted in and out of sleep but woke up each time she heard any noise.

She finally fell asleep hard. Her dream was a flutter of colors flashing past her. She walked down a road, and the faster she walked, the faster the colors fluttered. There were pictures of a tiger and a horse that flashed by. She started to run towards a large mansion. She reached for the gate's latch. As her fingers wrapped around the handle, everything disappeared – the house, the colors, and the pictures. She was falling through the darkness and landed in a lake with a splash. There was a woman in the lake. She was beautiful with flowing hair, and as the girl paddled towards her, the beautiful woman's skin turned green, and her hair turned to snakes. The woman screamed a high-pitched noise that made the girl's ears bleed. The girl jumped up out of her sleep in a sweat. She was panting hard. Fig watched her from the edge of their haystack with a puffed-out tail, a bewildered look on his face. "Sorry," she breathed.

The night continued with light sleep, the clouds outside creating shadows across the ceiling of the barn. It creaked and whined as the wind blew against it. She slowly pets the little orange cat who slept on her stomach. All she wanted to do was rest a full night through.

Fig suddenly lifted his head; his hair was standing on end. He started a deep throaty growl as he watched an unknown object moving around outside the window. She slowly raised herself to her elbows. She heard the scratching move around the building to the front of the barn. She slowly moved from her bed of hay to the door. She peered through the cracks of the door. Her heart rose into her throat when she heard the scratching get closer to where she was standing. She watched for a few moments in fear, and then she saw a large object move closer to the door.

It was a small horse, one that she had seen running through the field earlier that day. She heaved a great sigh of relief as the adrenaline slowed through her veins. She unlocked the door, and the horse came into the barn, walked over to a stall, and lay down in the hay. She relocked the door and walked over to it. The horse was tan in color with a golden mane that almost reached the ground. She placed a hand on its nuzzle and looked into the horse's eyes. It seemed to stare into her soul as if it knew the meaning of everything in the world. She almost felt hypnotized. Fig let out a gentle meow from their makeshift bed, and the girl shook herself out of the trance. She walked back over to their bed and lay back down to sleep.

Morning finally came as the sun reflected through the broken windows and made refracted rainbows fill the barn. She folded up her blankets and unlocked the door. The little horse ran out towards the field she had seen it in before. She walked over to the house and knocked on the door. Flynn was up and cooking something that smelled like cinnamon and apples over the fire.

"Morning," he said to her in a deep voice. "The wife is not home yet, but I reckon you two are hungry." Flynn put a saucer of milk down on the mat for Fig. The cat purred as he happily lapped it up. He handed her a bowl of porridge.

"There was a little horse that came to the barn last night," she told Flynn.

The little old man smiled at her, but clearly, the smile masked his genuine emotions. "I used to have a lot of horses and other animals too. The fences broke one night, and everyone left. The horses come back at night sometimes to sleep. I usually leave the door open for them so that they can get in," he explained, looking despondently out the window.

"I'm sorry to hear that! How did the fence break?" she asked; the disrepair outside began to make sense as she studied the small man's frail form and his weathered face.

"We had a terrible storm one night a few months ago. The lightning was firing so often that the sky was bright more often than it was dark. The booming thunder shook the house, too. When it was finally over in the morning, we went outside to find all the crops destroyed, and the animals had escaped. When you're done eating your breakfast, I'll show you," he told her with a tear in his eye.

"That's horrible!" the girl exclaimed. "I can't even imagine what that has done to you." Flynn nodded in response; he didn't seem to know what to say to her.

They walked out to the yard to look at what was left of the fence. It was broken in more than one spot. The stone posts were still intact. However, the wooden beams running between were damaged in some places. She looked closer at the beams to see scratch marks in the wood. She saw the same marks on the side of the barn. "That's why I told you to keep the door locked," Flynn said to her. "I don't know what came through with the storm, but it was not happy about our fence."

As they stood there examining the fence, a small woman came riding down the road on the back of a little golden horse. "There's my bride," Flynn said, the twinkle in his eye returning. Eleonore had long blonde hair wrapped up on top of her head. She was a plump woman with a scarlet shawl draped about her shoulders. You definitely could not miss her coming down the road. She had a bundle of wool attached to her bag and other goods such as fruits and vegetables in a basket on the horse's back.

"My sweet Eleonore, I've missed you," greeted the little man.

The little lady smiled sweetly back at her husband. "Hello, love," she replied. Her voice was sweet and airy like a bird's song on a breeze. "We have company," Eleonore stated as her husband helped her down off the horse. "Oh, it's you, dearie!

How are you? I haven't seen you in so long!" The little woman only came up to the girl's waist. She ran up to a girl and hugged her tightly.

With tears in her eyes, she hugged Eleonore back. "Do you remember me?" the girl said with a crack in her voice.

Eleonore stepped back to look up at the girl's face. "Why, of course, I do!" Eleonore chimed back.

"She doesn't remember who she is, Eleonore. She was hoping you could shed some light for her," Flynn explained.

Eleonore's face twisted to one of concern, "Are you two having a bit of fun by me?" Eleonore questioned. "Your name is Thea, you silly girl! Of course, I know who you are!" Eleonore started into Thea's eyes.

Thea sniffled and started to cry. Her shoulders heaved as she sobbed. Eleonore pulled her down to sit on the edge of a nearby bench and wrapped her arms around the crying girl.

"Do you not remember anything?" Eleonore asked. Thea shook her head.

Eleonore and Thea sat inside as Thea recapped all of her memory and what she had found. "Well, I know you live in a cabin off by yourself, but I'm not sure where that is, dear," Eleonore said regarding her home. "You always said you liked it off on your own so that you could grow your herbs. You started to come to the market about six months ago, and then about two months ago, you stopped coming. That sweet little cat there seemed lost without you. He continued to come to the market and sit at your empty stall, meowing at everyone that walked by."

Thea was puzzled and had no memories of any of this. She

didn't remember Eleonore or the market. "Do you know my family? Or who they are?" Thea asked.

"No dear, I'm sorry. You never talked about your family. You always changed the subject when someone asked you about them. Just you and your cat and your healing herbs."

Thea learned that she healed many people in the surrounding areas with the herbs sold in the market. She also knew that she had helped Eleonore with her booth and her wares. Eleonore weaved blankets and other items to sell in the market. She showed Thea her spinning wheel, which she had in the corner where she spun her fibers to weave; she also cleaned houses in town.

Thea continued to tell her story as she was walking towards Eleonore and Flynn's house. "I saved a fairy and then was welcomed by their group in the woods. I'm not sure how many days…"

"You were with the fairies?!" Eleonore interrupted her story, "And they allowed you to live?"

Thea had a confused look on her face. "Why, yes. I helped them protect their land from the elves."

Eleonore appeared very concerned with that new information. "The fairies don't live down this road," Eleonore said as she pointed out the window to the road Thea had come down. "That is the elves' land. You helped the fairies keep the land that they stole from the elves."

Thea was shocked. The thought never occurred that she wasn't helping the creatures that were doing good. "But I thought I was helping." She said in a weak voice.

"Not everything is how you perceive it, dearie. There are always two sides to a story; remember that," Eleonore instructed Thea.

"How did your herbs help the fairies?" Eleonore asked as she slowly sipped her tea.

"I didn't give them any herbs," Thea responded. "I'm not actually sure how I helped them." Thea rubbed her head as she tried to remember.

"What did you do then?" Eleonore inquired.

"Well, I scooped them up in my hand like this," Thea made a scooping motion, "and then….I nursed them to health." She said in a stutter as she saw the twisted expression on Eleonore's face. Thea brought the subject back to her faulty memory to avoid discussing what the fairies had called her magic.

The women continued to talk about what they could piece together and what questions Thea still had. "I just wanted to find another human to help me. Or at least to tell me who I am and where I belong."

Eleonore laughed as Thea said that statement to her. "Oh dearie, we're not humans." As her smile widens on her lips, Eleonore continued to chuckle. "Remember, dearie; not everything is as it seems."

Chapter Six

"What do you mean you're not humans?" Thea asked the little woman nervously.

"We're Brownies," Eleonore stated matter-of-factly. "Let me see that Book of Creatures you were talking about."

Thea pulled out the book and handed it to Eleonore. She flipped through the book and found the page of brownies. Thea read the information, learning that they were similar to elves, clean houses, and work with metal. There was a drawing of a man who looked similar to Flynn. All of the magic that came with the brownies had to do with the house's functioning and maintenance. Eleonore agreed with the majority of things on the page. "We used to do all of these things," she said with a melancholy smile. "About a hundred years ago, when we were still young enough to move around that well."

Thea spent the afternoon snacking on sweet baked treats with Eleonore, learning more about the Brownies. Eleonore told her how she cleans houses for the humans in town and dresses as a human. "Not everything is as it seems, dearie."

Thea then ventured out to help Flynn mend the broken fence. She helped the old man lift new timbers across the stone supports. The little brownie made new metal supports for the wall that looked to be strong and elegant. By supper time, they had the south side of the fence completed with new reinforcements.

The three of them sat at the table and dined on pork and fresh vegetables. Fig sat at the fireplace lazily lapping up milk from the saucer. They made plans to fix the fence and round up all of the animals roaming in the woods. Eleonore had collected some seeds and leaves to replant their gardens. They helped

Thea fix up the barn for her to stay a bit since Thea had offered to help the Brownies fix up their home.

Days passed quickly. Flynn and Thea rebuilt the entire fence and reinforced the woodwork with a beautiful cast iron picket. Eleonore spent the majority of her days out in their field replanting seeds, sowing the land.

"Good idea leaving the gate open last night. Some of the animals have made their way back to the barn," Thea sleepily reported as she sipped her tea by the fire. Over the previous night, a few of the horses had wandered back to the barn, along with a cow and a pair of pigs.
"The last thing we need to do is build a chicken coop, and then we should be back to normal around here," Flynn stated happily. "I think that's one thing I can handle on my own."

"It's Tuesday, dearie. We had better get moving," Eleonore said to Thea.

"Where are we going?" Thea questioned.

"We need to go to the market today. I have blankets to sell," the little brownie woman wrapped her head with a green scarf and slowly made her way to the barn. Thea collected her bag and helped the little woman onto a horse with her heaps of hand-woven blankets on the back. Thea mounted a golden horse herself, and small Fig perched up onto her shoulder. They rode down the dirt road, headed to the east, through the dark forest.

Thea kept seeing glimpses of sparkling shimmers through the trees. Eleonore noticed them too, "Better keep moving, dearie. There are always beautiful things, but dangerous too."

Thea felt the uncomfortable tingle of being watched as they continued down the path. Fig watched little frogs bounce through the grass and little fairies buzz overhead. If she hadn't already known what they were, Thea would have assumed they were hummingbirds. A horse ran across the path in front of them. It was white with a flowing mane that shined like silver. The little horse had a small horn growing from the middle of its head. Eleonore stopped her mount and pointed to a few strands of the snowy mane stuck on a bush.

"Get that!" she cried with excitement. "I'm sure you can use that with your healings." Thea hopped down from the horse and collected the stands, putting them into her bag. The texture felt smoother than normal horsehair and was cold to the touch. She hopped back on the horse, picking Fig up by the scruff of his neck, and placed him back on her shoulder. They started again to the market.

The market was a bright-colored array of booths. There were hundreds of people in well-pressed clothes, walking from stall to stall, buying and trading their wares. The women were in flowing dresses and the men in pressed linens.

Eleonore walked Thea over to an empty, dusty booth. "This is your booth, dearie," she said. The booth had months' worth of dust covering it; a faded sign said "Tonics" across the top. Behind the counter, there was a cabinet closed with an old lock. She tugged on it a few times, and it wouldn't budge. She remembers she carried an old key with her that Thea had discovered in her bag when she first woke up at the bank. After some rummaging, she found it. She stuck it in the lock, which groaned as she turned the key.

Inside, she found clothes, dried herbs, flowers, and small vials filled with different liquids; each had a little handwritten label attached to the bottle's neck with a piece of twine. She had bottles for pain relief, colds, and even a bottle marked "love spell. Fig walked over to his little cat bed in the back, by a blue chair, which looked like the one Thea had back home, only without the dingy buttons, and curled up for a nap. Thea spent the better part of an hour dusting off her booth and studying all the items locked in her cabinet; she was cross-referencing everything to her book and relearning what it all was.

She also found a silver key with a knotted design along the top, with a purple ribbon attached to it. She promptly put this with her other key in her bag. As she looked at the bottles, she saw one that had another tattered piece of paper that matched the other in her purse. It said, "Beware the woman with the flame tattoo…." Apprehension coursed through her veins. *Who had written the notes? What was she supposed to do if she met 'the woman with the flame tattoo?'* disquiet thoughts filled her head.

She saw Eleonore set up her booth across the way; she was doing business with a tall woman with long flowing red hair. She shook herself from her reverie and opened up for business. Thea sold a few items, stumbling through the transactions. Her prices must have been the same for some time as people seemed to simply hand her coins for items that they had bought before. Many of the clients asked her where she had been. Thea would respond with a vague "Oh, just traveling" as she put the gold coins into her bag.

As the day went on, Thea bought some cheese and wine from a booth and brought lunch over to Eleonore. The two munched on their meal, watching people walking by. Eleonore pointed out the women she used to clean for. "Oh, she has a huge house with nothing in it. It's beautiful from the outside, but she can't afford anything to fill it with. She never has her friends over and always says her husband is away on business… she doesn't have a husband. She keeps up the appearance, though. The one with the brown wavy hair there in the purple dress," she said gesturing. "She cooks the most wonderful food." Eleonore continued going through the crowd and smiled, watching Thea trying to remember everyone that she should have recognized. A few people walked up to

Thea's booth. She wiped her mouth and excused herself to assist them.

"Hello," Thea said to the woman. "How can I help you?" The woman was an average size wearing a pair of knee-length pants and dark black boots with a clean white shirt. Her skin was a beautiful hue of caramel, and her eyes were bright blue. She had chocolate brown hair loosely tied with a ribbon over her shoulder.

I'm looking for some rosewater, please," the woman said impatiently.

"Just a moment," Thea responded, slightly put off by the woman's curt attitude, as she shuffled through the cabinet. She found a bottle labeled "rosewater"; the pink liquid was almost transparent in the sunlight. She turned back to the woman and unsuccessfully tried to wipe the unease off her face. By this Time, Fig had jumped up on the counter and watched the woman very closely; his hair on his tail started to rise. Thea placed it on the counter next to him and took the five gold pieces that the woman had left for her. "Thank you for your business," Thea said with a falsely cheery smile.

"You don't recognize me, do you?" the woman questioned.

Thea looked at the woman for a moment and tilted her head to the side.

"No, I'm sorry. Have we met?" Thea asked hesitantly. The woman lowered her chin and smirked at Thea. Fig stood up, all of his hair on end. He let out a deep growl. She leaned in closer to Thea and whispered to her.

"We've been looking for you, Thea." Suddenly, the woman with the caramel skin turned in a circle and changed into a dark crow that flew into the sky, screeching ominously over the village.

Thea stood, amazed, staring at the sky where the crow had been. Terrified, Thea looked over to Eleonore to see if she had witnessed what just happened. Eleonore was pale as if she had only seen a ghost when she darted over to Thea's booth. Thea and Fig ran over to Eleonore, wide-eyed. "Who was that?!" Thea stammered.

"A witch," Eleonore said in a hushed whisper. Eleonore looked back and forth down the street and saw the other people whispering and pointing towards them.

"She said they were looking for me," Thea said in a small voice. Eleonore's eyes got big and full of fear.

"You better go hide, dearie. A witch looking for you is never a good sign. Head towards the far path, not back towards Flynn."

Thea, full of fear, went back to her booth and quickly packed up her bag with the bottles she had in her cabinet and a few of the herbs. She now had a heavy load full of bottles and gold coins. Locking what she couldn't carry into the cabinet, Thea had her booth closed up in a matter of minutes. She hurriedly bought some meat, cheese, and bread from a few vendors, though the people didn't seem eager to help her after seeing the Witch. Everyone seemed scared of her now. She hugged Eleonore and thanked her for her help as Eleonore responded with a quick pat and rushed push.

The cat led the way out of town into the dense woods. She couldn't figure out how the Witch knew her or what she could have done to cause a witch to be hunting her. She heard a crow cry in the distance, which made her heart jump up into her throat.

Thea and Fig continued to head west, away from her brownie friends and away from her cabin. Now that she had seen a woman turn into a crow, she had no idea what or who she could trust. *Eleonore sure seemed keen to be rid of me. I'm sure she was just worried for Flynn…* Thea pondered her new 'friend.'

They walked well past dusk and were stumbling through the underbrush in the darkening woods. Her eyes were heavy. She had had to pick up her sleepy feline and carry him; she knew she could not continue further tonight. She was lost deep in the woods; at least, she hoped that the Witch wouldn't be able to find her so far off the path. Thea made a lean-to with some tree branches and one of her blankets. She wished she could start a fire but didn't want to bring attention to her location, so she pulled some of the meat she had bought at the market out of her bag and snuggled up with Fig to eat their dinner.

Thea found she was just too unsettled to eat, however, and set her meat next to Fig instead. *Why is this all happening to me? What did I do to deserve this?* she sniveled to herself. She wondered if she had done something to warrant this. It would be hard to argue since she still couldn't remember anything. *But who was this Witch, and who was the 'they' she had mentioned?*

Where am I going to go now? Who can I trust, who can I talk to? The thoughts were running through her head faster than Willow spoke to her back at the fairy circle.

She pulled out her book of medicine and herbs, as well as the Book of Creatures, and started to read by moonlight. Maybe there would be a clue in her books. She was desperately trying to get a grasp on what was going on around her. Every day she seemed to be left with more questions than answers.

"I'm really tired of not sleeping in a bed," she said to her furry faced friend. Fig looked as if he could not care less. He was curled up on Thea's lap, ready to go to sleep. They moved into their lean-to and made a bed with leaves and her blanket. Thea was terrified and didn't want to sleep, but her body was giving out on her. The exhaustion was taking over as she fought the heaviness of her eyelids. They laid down by the base of the tree, and though her will was fighting for the energy to stay awake, her body drifted off to sleep.

She finally had a dreamless night and woke up feeling rested. Her head was not pounding, and the gentle warmth from the sun made her feel comfortable as she shook Fig awake from his slumber. She explored the surrounding area of trees, looking for her way back to a path. She saw a field a little way off through the edge of the forest. It was covered in large golden faced sunflowers. The bright, cheery, yellow flowers seemed to be turning their faces towards the sun, soaking up the warmth as well. Thea was ecstatic to be leaving the harshness of the underbrush and being back in the sun. The openness of the field looked welcoming, just the amount of cheerfulness she needed. Not being able to remember anything and knowing now that witches are looking for her, Thea didn't know what to trust. She was looking for comfort. "Let's go look at the flowers, sweet boy," she said to Fig as she reached under his chin with a scratching finger.

The two got up and made their way to the field. The birds were singing a happy tune, and it got warmer the farther out of the trees they went. The grass was longer there and met Thea about calf-high. As Thea and Fig walked, there was a flurry of blue feathers and squawking beneath their feet. They both jumped into the air with fright. Fig had stirred up a nest of peacocks as he trotted about the grass. Thea laughed at her curious companion when his fur stood up with surprise. She picked up one of the feathers that were drifting down through the air and fixed it in her raven hair. With an extra bounce in their step, the two made it to the field of flowers that were taller than Thea by at least a head's length. She smiled again, a happy, familiar feeling rushing over her.

She was in a daze as they walked through the flowers. Thea tripped on something, landing hard on her palms and knees.

"Ouch!" Thea yelled.

She rolled over and wiped the dirt from her hands, and dusted off her knees. She looked back at her feet to see what she had hit. Thea saw a small house that was no higher than her ankle, with a smashed roof. She saw a little man dressed all in green, with a pointed hat, run deep into the field.

"Oh! Sorry!" Thea called out after him.

Fig started to run towards the little man in hot pursuit.
"Fig! Let him be!" Thea yelled after him. The little orange cat stopped and slowly sulked back to Thea.

She sat up with her knees bent and attempted to put the roof back on the little house. "I hope that helps," she called out to the little man who had stopped and was watching from the thicket of flowers. She looked around the flowers' base and saw more small houses with more little faces watching from the windows in dread. "We won't be bothering you," Thea said to the tiny houses as she waved at them innocently. She scooped up the cat and continued on her way.

"Watch where you step seems to be sound advice," Thea said to Fig. The cat turned and looked her in the face; he tilted his head to the side and responded with a sweet meow.

The pair continued through the field of flowers, the trees were starting to come into view, and back into the woods, they were headed. Thea had no idea where they were going, but Fig seemed confident on where he was walking. She followed mindlessly, pondering where she may have come from and where she may have met the Witch before. The forest foliage grew thicker the deeper they went into the woods.

Thea started to feel as though they were being watched again. She saw the glowing eyes of beings unknown off in the distance, which seemed to disappear when eye contact was made. Thea felt on edge and unnerved. She hoped she was overreacting. With no other choices, they walked until they found a brick road that ran north to south. There was a directional sign with arrows pointing either way. To the left, the jaunty, hand-painted sign in bright colors stated, "Dragon's Tooth Lake," and to the right, in the splintered wood was etched, "Monkey Tree Village."

"Well, Fig?" she questioned her little cat. "Where are we headed to?" They both paused for a moment with their heads cocked to one side, indecisive looks upon their faces.

"Meow." Fig stood up from where he sat and started to walk down the road to the left.

"The happy-looking sign is what did it for me too," she said with relief as she quickly followed after her cat friend in a hurried step, away from the more ominous sign.

She heard the cackle of a crow far off in the distance coming from behind them. This caused a shiver to run down her spine as she quickly looked over her shoulder, and they walked a little faster down the road. The heels of her boots were lightly clicking on the bricks. *Click-clack, click-clack* down the road. She walked more quickly to try to catch up to the swift cat. Then she heard it: Click-click*, clack-clack*. There were extra footsteps on the road. Without slowing her steps, Thea looked over her shoulder to see a cloaked figure walking behind her. Her heart started to beat faster as she walked. Picking up her pace, Thea started to pass the cat. "Let's go, Fig. We're being followed."

The stranger had also picked up their pace, walking faster

down the road. Thea went from a fast walk to a sprint, then started to run, with Fig in tow. Her hood fell back, and her hair was dancing in the wind behind her. Her chest was pumping hard as she panted; sweat was rolling down her brow. She ran and ran, but the figure kept in stride. Her headache started to rage behind her eyes. Just when she thought she could run no more, the footsteps suddenly stopped behind her. She slowed her pace and looked over her shoulder. Fig was the only being insight.

Thea scooped up Fig and stepped off the brick path into a thicket. She bent over and rested her hands on her knees as she heaved, trying to catch her breath and not puke after running so far. She couldn't see any sign of the cloaked individual as she peered out of the trees and down the road. Thea yanked her cloak off from around her neck; feeling suffocated and warm, she stuffed it in her bag. She was in a panic as she didn't know why this person started to chase her.

Was that the Witch? Where did they go? What am I supposed to be doing? Thea shut her eyes as these questions raced through her brain. She started letting out long breaths from her mouth as she was trying to calm her heartbeat.

When she popped her head out of the trees, she saw an empty road that leads down to the blue waters of a lake. Within a few minutes, they were standing on the bank, looking at the clear water. At least the run got them down to the path quickly; she kicked off her shoes and waded in the cool water. Still, she continued to look back at the road on edge, expecting to see the cloaked figure, but there was nothing there but the bricks. Fig sat on the bank and slowly lapped up the water as he watched Thea pace back and forth. She was still hot from her unexpected run but couldn't tell if the sweat was from exertion or nerves. She dropped her bag next to the cat and jumped fully into the water, diving down to the deep end of the lake, trying to cleanse her detailed thoughts. She treaded water and pushed her hair back out of her face.

"Be careful of the Water Nymphs; they don't like it when you swim in their lake," a soft voice said from the bank. She slowly turned around to where she had left Fig. The cloaked figure was sitting on the bank, with Fig on her lap – purring and showing his stomach up to the air to be scratched. Thea's panic showed on her face. "Thea? Why are you looking at me like that?" The voice was a whimsical song that floated through the air. Thea squinted at the cloaked figure as she pushed the hood back.

The girl was on the bank, with her legs crossed out in front of her. Fig clearly seemed to know who she was as he was purring and nudging her hand with his head. The girl had the same green eyes, and round face as Thea but had fiery red hair that glowed in the sunshine. "Thea! It's Robin; why are you looking at me so crazy?" Robin yelled out to Thea as she pushed back the hood to better reveal her face.

"I'm sorry," Thea said softly, "I don't remember you," she stated with complete hesitation. The fear was back and rising into her throat.

The girl stared back at Thea blankly. "Thea, I'm your best friend; how can you say you don't remember me?"

Chapter Seven

Thea climbed out onto the bank, sopping wet. Robin got up from where she was sitting, ran over to Thea, and wrapped her arms around Thea's waist, hugging her tightly. "I haven't seen you for months! I didn't know what happened to you." Robin rested her head on Thea's shoulder as she hugged her. Thea stood there with the water running down her face, her arms hanging limp at her sides.

She had been so confused and scared that she didn't know how to respond. Could Thea even trust that this girl was her friend?

"I'm sorry,…Robin? I don't know you," Thea said sternly. She blankly stared at the redhead, who looked hurt as she slowly moved away.

"How can you say that?" Robin asked in a soft voice that cracked at the end of the question.

Fig continued to rub against Robin's legs as if he were trying to tell Thea he knew her. Thea tilted her head to the side and was fighting back her tears of frustration. She didn't know what to believe anymore.

"What do you mean you don't remember? What has happened to you?" Robin asked in a concerned tone. "You told me that you were leaving to go to the market one day, and then, you never came back. I went to your cabin, and you were just gone. People said the Kingdom of Owls kidnaped you. I've been so worried..." Robin's voice trailed off at the end of her thought.

Thea stared through her, for the moment distracted from her history. Off in the distance of the forest, she was watching a shadow move through the trees. "I have to go," Thea said slowly as she watched the shadow disappear.

Robin looked over her shoulder towards the trees. She saw the shadowy figure coming towards them too.

"Trust me. Please, come with me," Robin said urgently.

Not sure if she should trust Robin but positive that she didn't want to confront the shadow, Thea nodded. The two women grabbed their things from the bank and jogged back to the road.

"My home is just down the way," Robin said in a breathy voice.

The shadowy form had made it to the edge of the trees and was headed towards the lake. Its mass was growing, as if it were engulfing everything around it, drawing everything into its darkness. The air turned cold and burned their lungs as they ran down the road. Fig growled as he darted ahead of the girls. The cat undoubtedly knew where they were going as he veered off the main road and down an unmarked path. Thea started to panic; it was harder to breathe, and her head was pounding at her temples.

There was a house in the opening of the trees at the end of the path. Thea didn't look back again but pushed to make it to the house. They ran through the door, and Robin threw the latch. They fell into a pile on the floor, heaving chests and sweat running down their faces. Fig stared at the door, growling with his fur on end. Thea held her breath and listened. She heard the same slow scratch on the porch's wooden floor that she had heard in the dark at her cabin. The air was frigid, and the hair on the back of Thea's neck was standing on end. She looked to her right and saw Robin slowly getting up and grabbing a sword from the side of the door. She put a finger to her lips to signal Thea to stay quiet. Robin rose to the window ledge and peeked out to her porch. Her eyes got large with fear as she backed away from the window with small half steps. "Grimalkin…." She hissed out in a breath. Robin raised her sword above her head and waited, her focus on the door. Thea froze and stared at the woman with a vacant gloss over her eyes.

Scratch.

Scratch.

Scratch.

"Grab that," Robin motioned with her head to a wooden staff next to the bookcase. "Thea! Grab that!" Robin hissed at her. Thea took a deep breath and shuddered herself back to reality as she cautiously grabbed the staff. She was beyond terrified. She looked over at Robin and followed suit by raising her staff in the same way.

"Open the door," Robin mouthed to Thea.

Before them stood a sizeable hazy figure that looked like a cat but was a horse's size; it filled the doorway. The shadow bent its head down and peered into the house. The eyes were fiery red and burned through Thea's soul; she was frozen in her place, full of fear. Thea had a flash of surreal memory, of being consumed by a lion-like figure in a whirlwind of thick black smoke, spinning around her, and had seeped into her mouth. She then started to levitate. Thea felt a sharp pain in her temple; she then shook herself back to the present threat. Robin lunged forward, plunging her blade into the shadow; her red hair blew back with force, and she had to squint her eyes; the shadow evaporated into a mist. There was a cackle of laughter off in the distance, followed by the cry of a crow. The two girls looked at each other, gasping for air.

Robin smirked at Thea. "Never a dull moment in Erresuma."

Chapter Eight

Thea crumpled into herself by the bookcase, trying to catch her breath. After a moment, she looked around her surroundings, trying to soak it all in. She noticed a small painting framed on the shelf; Thea and Robin smiled on a bench. Thea took the picture into her hand and studied it. She smiled.

"Do you believe me now?" Robin asked as she dropped down beside her. Robin fluffed her skirt as she crossed her legs under her. "I've known you my whole life, Thea. I can't believe you don't know who I am." She looked into Thea's eyes with tears filling them. Robin took Thea's hand, and they sat there looking at the picture.

Thea finally felt at ease for the first time since she had met Robin and started to relax a bit. "The shadow thing…" Thea stated.

"The Grimalkin?" Robin refined.

"Yeah… I think it's been following me."

Robin looked at Thea with a slightly irritating smirk. "Thea, that thing has been terrorizing Erresuma for years. I have never seen it before" Thea had the same confused look on her face that she got whenever she tried to remember anything; the fuzziness that appeared instead of her memory always brought the splitting headache.

"Do you want me to tell you the story of the Grimalkin?" Robin asked. Thea looked at her wide-eyed and nodded slowly, as a little child would when asked if they wanted to hear a bedtime story. Robin jumped up to her feet and offered her friend a hand up, leading her over to the couch and went into the kitchen. Robin poured a fizzy drink out of the icebox. "Here you go. Get comfortable." Thea took a sip of the Dandelion Fizz; it tasted sweet with the syrup that Robin had added, like dandelion tea but with a sparkling bubble that tickled her nose. Robin stood in the middle of the sitting area, preparing to put on a production. Robin kicked her slippers off to the side and cleared her throat.

"' The story of the Grimalkin' otherwise known as 'The terror of Lilly Quinn,'" she started with a dramatic flair. "Once upon a time, there was a young girl named Lilly Quinn, who was half-elf and half-human. She grew up in Erresuma's kingdom of Starling with her mother – as her father was an elf and lived in his rightful kingdom. She was the most beautiful girl, with long ringlets of blonde hair and memorizing, grey eyes. Her ears and her nose had a slight point to them resembling her elvish father. Her mother was accused of being a witch as her mother was before her....and her mother before her. They lived on the outskirts of Starling, where they had a small farm near the kingdom of the elves. Lilly was often alone; her elf family did not accept her because she was not a pure elf, and her human family did not accept her because of the elf's blood. All she had was her mom." Robin twisted her face around to make a disgusted look. "Lilly grew up to be quite stunning; people would stare at her in awe when she would go by. Lilly never understood the stares; she'd blush and run and hide; she did not have any social interactions with anyone besides her mother.

Well, one day, Lilly's mom died. Just died. No one knows why, but the neighbors found her laying down by the creek like she had been taking a nap, but she was dead." Robin shrugged her shoulders, and she shook her head. "Lilly was only about twelve years old at the time, and she went to stay with her human aunts. It was around that Time that Lilly started to find that she was different from other people. She had a gift. She could change shapes and become animals. Her cousins could do it as well, although the people of the kingdom didn't suspect them of being witches, as they never claimed to be related to Lilly or her mother.

Lilly was special. She could change to more animals than the others, but, more impressively, she could also manipulate fire." Robin made a gesture of shooting fireballs from her hands as she danced around the center of the room. Fig watched her dance back and forth from Thea's lap. "Her aunts were witches, her cousins were witches, the whole family was witches, but Lilly was the most powerful Witch. Instead of connecting with her family, she grew vain hearing everyone say how beautiful and powerful she was. Now the rule of shapeshifters is that they can change to that animal eight times without a problem, but if they do it a ninth time, they become that animal forever. Well, Lilly found a way around that magic, somehow. She fell in love with changing into a cat, but not just any cat – she became the large black cat known as the Grimalkin. In that form, she had glowing eyes and a white patch on her chest. The story goes that Lilly was still lonely, even after she finally was allowed to join her family; she had never learned how to talk to anyone socially. Her extended family resented her beauty, power, and vanity." Robin emphasized her story with dramatic gestures and expressions; Thea was enraptured. "When Lilly would get bored, she would change into a cat and watch people in through their windows; she would pretend that she was part of their world. As Time went on, Lilly became stronger and more powerful; her family became jealous of her. Her cousins would tell her that her beauty was failing the older she became. They were just downright mean to her."

"While in town one day with her cousins, they tripped her in the marketplace, and she fell into a pigpen. She was covered in filth! The whole town was laughing at her, telling her that she was 'ugly as a pig.'"

"Well, Lilly finally had enough of her cousins being cruel to her and launched a fireball right at their heads." Robin fell backward as if acting out, missing a giant fireball from the sky. "The market caught on fire and burnt to the ground, ruining everyone's booths – a few people even died. The town now had confirmation of the family being witches. Lilly fled and hid in the forest as the town's people started a mob to look for her. Lilly Quinn changed into the Grimalkin and never looked back. Her vanity became so deep that she found a spell that kept her youth intact by devouring the souls of people. She never changed back from being in her cat form. She had been hiding for so long, she forgot how. She has been hunting throughout the land for hundreds of years, hunting down the most beautiful or powerful people in order to eat their souls and stay alive." Robin took a bow. "And that is the story of the Grimalkin. Or as those of us who know the story, Lilly Quinn – the Witch."

After a moment of silence, while the story settled in, Thea questioned, "Why do you think she's stalking me?"

"She either wants your beauty or your powers," Robin said non-empathically. Thea raised her eyebrows at Robin.

"Oh, come on, Thea, you have both. You would be the perfect person for the Grimalkin to get." Robin said as she plopped down next to her.

"What do you mean about powers?" Thea asked.

"You don't remember anything, do you?" Robin asked. Robin leaned in really close to Thea's face. "Thea, you are a witch! You have powers." Robin had a broad smile across her face as she giggled.

"Wait....what?" Thea stammered. Fig nudged her hand and meowed.

Robin got up and grabbed a spellbook that she put in Thea's hands. "You. Are. A. Witch."

Chapter Nine

Thea and Robin spent the entire night, into the wee hours of the morning, sharing the last few weeks' experiences. Robin told Thea stories about how they met while working in the market when they were still in school and how Thea had healing powers. Robin, too, was a witch, though she did not have the same level of abilities as Thea. Thea learned that she had lived with her aunt since a young age, but Robin did not know what had happened to Thea's family.

Robin had many spellbooks and books on herbs. "I feel like I've been walking around with this blank stare on my face. Everything feels so surreal to me." Thea said as she thumbed through a book of healing potions. "I don't remember any of this business." Thea looked up to catch Robin's gaze. She had her head tilted to the side and had a concerned look on her face. Thea grabbed her temple as her head started to throb again. She looked over Robin's shoulder towards the trees, a blank expression on her face. The red-headed woman slowly backed out of her embrace and looked Thea square in the eye. "What's wrong with you?"

Who is this? Fig seems to know her and is fine with her. Thea's lips were slightly parted as she started to speak but then abruptly stopped.

"Here, Lady," Robin said as she tossed a small vial at Thea. "Rub that on your temples and take a couple of deep breaths." Thea popped the cork and ran the vile under her nose; the sweet aroma of peppermint came pouring out. "It will calm the pain. And, chew on this eucalyptus leaf." Robin pulled out a leaf from a pouch on a shelf. "It also helps with colds," Robin said with a wink. Almost instantly, Thea felt better, and her head felt clear; the pain had subsided.

"Well, Lady, I don't know what happened to you, but if the Grimalkin is stalking you, we better have you study up on your spells....and maybe on how to defend yourself. You looked like you were going to pass out yesterday."

The two girls sat out in the grass with a stack of books, reading about herbs and spells and creatures from far off lands. Fig was nearby, practicing his hunting skills by chasing the little critters that hid in the long grass. They drank dandelion wine and dandelion fizz as they lounged outside each day. Thea learned about her ability to heal and what all the herbs were that she had found in her bag. Thea, for the First Time that she could remember, didn't have a headache and felt calm. Fig seemed content as he grazed on catnip and laid amongst the books and parchments. It felt like a lazy summer vacation visiting someone's lake cabin – drinking, talking, and lazing out in the sun. Thea started to forget that there was a killer witch... Grimalkin....thing, stalking her. The two girls grew closer over the week as they shared laughs and taught each other things.

"Come on! Start!" Thea yelled at her hand. "Please start?" She had one finger on a line of a book as she held her other hand out in front of her. She was staring at her palm with an intensity as if she was watching an ant walk across her hand. She was getting mad that the spell was not working.

"I can't do this!" She yelled in frustration up to the sky.

"Ha! Sure, you can!" Robin laughed. "You just need to believe that you can." Robin picked Thea's hand up out of her lap and pressed the tip of her nail into Thea's palm. "Push all of your energy right...there," she said as she jabbed her nail down into Thea's palm.

"Ow! You slag!" Thea cursed as she shook her hand in pain.

"Just do it," Robin said with annoyance in her voice. "Here, shut your eyes and focus." She stated as she put her hand up over Thea's eyes.

"This is silly," Thea sighed.

"Just focus....then snap your fingers." Thea let out a sigh and let her shoulders relax down into a slump. "I guess you are too weak to do it," Robin mocked.

"Shut it, Robin." Thea focused on the pierced mark of her palm. She tried to will the blood in her body to push towards her palm. Thea then made one vigorous shake of her hand and snapped her fingers. To her shock and delight, a red flame appeared in her hand as a small orb. She raised it close to her face and stared at it wide-eyed. "Whoa. That's awesome." She whispered.

"I know, right?" Robin whispered back. Thea could see Robin's unfocused smile through the flame. Thea watched the flame for a few more seconds until her skin started to blister. She shook her hand in pain and sent the fireball flying off into the woods.

"Again," Robin said in an authoritarian tone. "You're getting so close."

Thea shook her head at her as she was shaking her burnt hand.

"That really hurt, and my skin is coming off my hand," Thea replied with a sulk.

"You HAVE TO keep going! This stuff is so important for you to learn!" Robin answered back to Thea. She moved closer to Thea and examined her burnt hand. "It will heal just fine, lady. You have to learn your magic. There is so much time to make up for!" Robin was trying to sound excited.

"Time to make up for? For what?" Thea looked at Robin with her head tilted to the side.

Robin paused for a second before continuing: "You were just so powerful before; we don't want you to be vulnerable anymore."

Thea gave Robin a look of disbelief but continued with making fireballs with her raw hand.

Why does she care so much? She knows how to do magic.

She continued practicing until her hand had started to bleed through the oozing blisters. Having had enough for one day, the girls retired, much to Robin's displeasure.

"Wake up!" Robin yelled. "We've got training to do."

Thea slowly rose from her bed up in the loft. "Why are you up already?" Thea questioned in the middle of a yawn. The sun was barely up over the horizon. Fig meowed in protest as Thea started to get out of bed. As she began to stumble down the stairs to the main level of the house, she had to duck; there was a staff flying through the air at her head!

"What the hell are you doing?!" she yelled at Robin.

"We've got training to do!" Robin squealed in happiness as she bounded from foot to foot, holding another staff in her hands. "Let's go!" Robin sprinted for the door.

Thea rolled her eyes at Robin's energetic bounce as she tied her hair up in a bun on top of her head. *There was no need to attack me*, she thought. She picked the staff up with her bandaged, blistered hand and slowly followed out the door behind Robin. The air was crisp, and the crickets were still chirping from behind the blades of grass. It was too early to be out of bed.

"Alright, Lady, let's see what you got." Robin had the staff held in both hands out in front of her. She lunged at Thea, who shrieked and blocked the attack with her own staff.

"Really?" Thea asked. "Why are we doing this?" She questioned as the wood cracked against each other.

Fig perched himself up in a window to watch the two dance through the field.

"You used to know how to do this, Thea," Robin grunted out in rushed breath as she spun in a circle and swung at Thea with an overhead attack. "You used to be good at this!" she hissed out as she swept Thea's legs out from under her.

Thea hit the ground with a loud thud, and her head bounced off the earth. "Ow!" Thea groaned as she grabbed the back of her head.

"Come on," Robin said as she held out her hand to help Thea up. "You have to learn this."

The girls continued to practice their moves as the sun came up and moved to the noon sky. They took a break for lunch, and Thea chewed on some more leaves to settle her pain. Her muscles ached, and her head was pounding again. Sandwiches of smoked ham and Gouda cheese were made – strawberries with chunks of dark chocolate for dessert. Fig lapped a bowl of cream at the end of the table. He sat there like he was people too.

"Are you ready for more, Thea?" Robin was braiding her hair, looking at Thea with wide-eyed curiosity.

"Um, no," Thea stated as she rubbed her lower back. "I think

I'm good with this for a while."

Robin seemed uneasy by this response. "Alright, we should do some more studying than. We've got to make sure you remember as much as you possibly can." Robin stated.

Thea was perplexed. The stuff they have been doing seemed to be for fun, up to this point. "Why are you so concerned about what I remember and what I can do?" Thea questioned. Her brow was furrowed.

Robin let out a soft sigh as she sat down and thought about where to start. "I just don't want to see you get hurt again." She replied carefully. "You need to be on top of your game in case Lilly comes back looking for you." Robin's answers were prolonged and carefully planned out. The look on her face was of guarded concern as she watched Thea's face to see how she was reacting to the statement.

"Why do I have the feeling that you are not telling me everything that you know?" Thea questioned as she stood to clear the plates to the sink.

Robin seemed to be torn with what was running through her head. Thea didn't know what to think as she studied her friend's face. "Why aren't you straight with me, Robin?" Thea's voice had turned stern, and the expression on her face harden. "What is going on here?"

Robin let out a soft sigh before she started to speak. "When I said I didn't know what had happened to you, it wasn't the full truth...." She trailed off as she spoke.

"You need to explain to me what you are talking about," Thea responded sternly. She could feel her face turning hot as she spoke to Robin.

"Lilly Quinn is following you around for a reason." She started softly.

"People said that she tried to eat your soul, like the other people that she has attacked over the years, but you were different....She couldn't defeat you or take your powers." Robin looked at Thea sheepishly as she spoke. "You were hunting her for most of your life. Lilly killed your parents and why you were living with your auntie when we were growing up. She ate their souls and stole their powers."

Thea felt all the blood drain from her face; she suddenly felt numb and empty inside. "What?" was all Thea could stammer out as a response. She leaned her body against the counter. "So, you are telling me that I am a witch that some super witch killed my parents, and I'm now a witch hunter? Really? This is my real life?" Thea's response came out with emotions mixed with disbelief and anger, behind a sarcastic laugh. She was infuriated that Robin had previously lied about the knowledge of her family. *Why is she telling me now that my family is dead when she had said she didn't know what happened to them?*

Robin pursed her lips and slowly nodded her head in agreeance. "People said that you finally stalked her like prey, outside of Starling Township about three months ago and attacked her with your fireball magic. She countered with her own purple fireball. When you two ran together and started to fight, there was a large explosion in the forest, and both of you disappeared into thin air. I had begged you to wait for me before you left to go find Lilly, but you are so stubborn; you were gone before I woke up that day."

Thea just stared at Robin. She was stunned with everything that had been going on and how she woke in the middle of nowhere, all by herself. It made sense to her that it was magic that caused all of this.

"You had even left Fig behind at my house; how he ever went out and tracked you down is beyond me. We all thought you two killed each other, but Lilly started hunting again. She is back to take one person a month… .it's been almost a month since her last known victim. That's why I'm pushing you to remember." Robin had hope in her eyes as she studied Thea's face. "You are the only one that has been known to be strong enough to survive her attack. The only one, Thea!" Robin walked over and wrapped her arm around Thea's waist. "We just need to figure out how to make you remember." Fig jumped up onto the counter and started to purr and nudge Thea's hand. She lifted her bandaged hand and scratched the little orange cat behind the ears.

The two sat on the couch, not speaking to each other. A small rainstorm had rolled in and was rhythmically tapping on the windows. Fig settled himself in between the two women and was showing his belly, looking for scratches.

"I know it is a lot of information to take in…." Robin started, "but you can't run from Lilly forever. You are stronger than she is; you just need to remember so that we can get her." Robin paused as if she was looking for some sort of acknowledgment from Thea.

"We?" Thea questioned back as she fiddled with a loose string on her skirt.

"I'm not letting you go out alone this time. I'm not as talented as you are, but I can help."

Thea looked up and met her eyes. She smiled. "I don't know where to start to get my memory back. It looks like we have been studying this stuff our whole lives, and now I'm expected to relearn it all in a few weeks." Thea said with a shrug.

Fig lifted his head from the couch. "Meow." He squeaked out

with a sleepy yawn. He jumped down and walked over to the stack of books on the floor. He nuzzled the pile until they all came crashing down.

"What are you doing, cat?" Thea questioned.

He started to paw at one of the books while mowing. She walked over to the mess the cat made and created to pick the books up. The book that Fig had been pawing at was navy blue leather and had a purple pentagram imprinted on the cover. Thea bent down and picked up the book. She ran her fingers over the surface and then noticed the lock with a knotted design on the binding. "Why is this book locked?" Thea asked Robin.

"I don't know; it's your book," Robin said as she walked over to examine the book with Thea. "Grab my bag, will ya?" Thea mumbled as she gestured to where it was hanging on the back of the chair.

Robin grabbed the bag and brought it over to where Thea had plopped down on the floor. "Thanks." Thea started to rifle through the collection of things she had found over the past few weeks. "Ah!" She exclaimed as she pulled out the small key that she had seen in her booth at the market.

It slid into the small rusted lock with surprising ease. She turned the lock, and the book flew open after being released from the tight hold of the binding. The pages flipped open to the middle of the book.; every page had drawings and writing in Thea's hand. A surge of energy ran through the book and into Thea's fingers. A green aura surrounded her and the book. Thea lifted her head from the book and looked at Robin, who was staring at her in horror. A smile spread across Thea's face as the green light slowly ran back into the book. "These are my spells," Thea said as she felt the power surge through her veins.

Her smile turned into a smirk. She liked the feeling that was taking over her body. The power made her feel amazing. Thea spent the night sitting by the fire flipping through her book of drawings and notes. She was trying to remember anything from her past. Thea found a spell that used almond and basil water, with arrowroot dust and an apple slice to clear up migraine headaches. She gave Robin the spell, who went into the kitchen to whip up a fresh batch to have on hand for Thea. She placed it into a vile and put it into her pantry to settle. Robin eventually faded off to her bedroom while Thea continued her studies.

She found a fiery flame sketch, with the caption "Flame Tattoo" written under the picture. She looked at her notes she has been collecting throughout her adventure.

"Flame tattoo, huh? Do you know what that means, Fig?" She asked through a yawn.

Her cat companion sat and stared at her with sleepy eyes. He gave her a soft meow and started to walk towards the loft, stopping to see if Thea would follow him to bed.

"Alright, you win, little man. Let's go to bed." The two made their way to the loft.

Thea slept hard through the night and didn't wake until the early afternoon. Her body was sore from all the training she was doing the day before. When she went down to the main level of the house, she realized that Robin had left. She fixed herself a bite to eat, then settled down on the couch with her book. She noticed there were about a hundred empty vials on the side table in a wooden crate. Thea's migraine was back. She went to the pantry and took a sip of the concoction that Robin had made last night. Her head felt clear, almost instantaneously.

"This stuff is awesome, Fig.," Thea said as she held the bottle up to look at the clear liquid.

Later, as Thea was busy practicing her conjuring of a fireball, Robin came in the door with a basket full of arrowroots. "That spell we did is awesome," Robin said with a wide smile on her face. "I went out and picked all of this, so we can make a bunch of it to sell at the market."

She dropped her basket on the table and started to tie strings around the roots to hang them from the ceiling beams so that the root could be dried.

The three of them ventured out to the garden and picked bunches of basil. Everything was still covered in a light dew from the late-night storm. The sun was trying to peek through the clouds. Thea had her face turned up to catch the little bit of sunshine when she heard a crow cry in the nearby trees. A shiver went down her spine, and she looked over at Robin. "Let's get into the house," Robin said as she picked up the last of her basil.

"Do you think it was the witch from the market?" Thea asked as they went inside.

"Well, if it's the woman you met before, and she is following you, I bet it's Lilly Quinn's cousin, Thalia," Robin said, as she was looking over her shoulder into the trees. The girls followed Fig into the house and latched the door behind them. It felt like it was going to be an indoor day, anyway.

"Why are we going to sell potions at the market?" Thea asked as she was fixing the basil to boil on the stove. "Well, you like to eat, right? We need money to continue to buy food." Robin replied.

"When I was at the market, Eleonore acted terrified of the

thought of a witch being there and following me. Won't they be scared of me if they know I'm a witch?" Thea seemed nervous to ask her that question.

Robin tilted her head back and let out a belly laugh at that question. "Well, when you, and the rest of them, though you were selling "MEDICINE," were they scared of you?"

Thea shook her head no in response.

"Well, you were a witch then; they just didn't know it." Robin pulled two mortars out of the cupboard. "People are scared of what they are ignorant about. There are always two sides to every person; to every opinion." Thea sat and nodded her head as she listened to what Robin was saying. "Sometimes, it is all how you spin it with people. By calling you a healer and having the town's people think you are just a girl that lives in the woods and collects herbs to make medicine, rather than the magical community that knows you are a witch, collecting herbs in the woods to make potions." Robin winked at Thea as she pulled a large sack of almonds out of her storage place.

The two girls ground the herbs and nuts in the mortars, as Fig lazily lounged by the fire. They were boiling the almonds and basil to make the waters needed for their potion. It would take a few days for the arrowroot to dry out enough to make it into a powder. Thea cut up pieces of apple and had them float in each bottle that they were getting ready for market. They started to make handwritten labels for the bottles when a soft plinking noise came from behind the stove.

"What is that?" Thea asked as she held her breath, trying to hear the sound.

Robin listened for a moment. "Oh! It's Patrick!" She said as she jumped up and rushed over to the cupboard next to the stove.

"Patrick?" Thea questioned as she watched Robin open the cupboard door.

Robin opened the cupboard door to reveal another door. It was cast iron with metalwork details of vines and flowers covering the exterior. Robin was down on her hands and knees, reaching into the small space to turn the latch. Inside was a gnome wearing what was once an elegant suit but was now faded with time. He was holding his hat in front of his chest. He had kind eyes that had a hint of sadness buried behind them.

"Sorry to bother you, Miss Robin, but I require your help! Ellie is sick and not responding to anyone. She won't wake up" His voice was deep and gravely.

"Oh Patrick, that is horrible! Please bring her in."

The little gnome, who was no bigger than Fig, came into the room through the cupboard door, carrying a much smaller Ellie in his arms. Robin laid out a blanket for Ellie to be placed on.

"You have a room behind your stove?" Thea questioned as she tried to look through the small door.

"Well, it's more of a small house back there." She stated back.
"It's a pleasure to meet you, Miss," Patrick said with a solemn bow of his head. Thea smiled and nodded to the little gnome.

Thea knelt next to her friend and looked at the little gnome's body. Ellie seemed labored as she breathed. Without speaking, Thea unbandaged her blistered hand without hesitation and held her hand palm down over Ellie, just as she had done before with fairies and elves. The energy from Thea could be seen pouring into Ellie's lifeless body; the dark mass of Ellie's sickness could be seen leaving her body and going into the fingertips of Thea. The seer power coming from Thea lit the room in a green hue that out powered the light coming from the lanterns above. Even Thea's hair looked green, as the force between her and the small gnome blew her hair into an unkempt mess.

The little gnome rose off the ground a then slowly drifted down like a leaf falling from a tree. Thea fell backward in a forceful jolt. Ellie gasped for air and then opened her eyes wide as she started to cough and choke on her own spit. Robin lifted her to a sitting position and slowly rubbed Ellie's back. "Are you ok, Ellie?" Robin asked. Ellie slowly nodded yes, as she was still coughing. "Are you?" Robin directed to Thea.

Thea was in shock, staring at the little gnome on the floor. Ellie was now alert and looking around the room while Patrick was hugging her. Thea started to cough. She coughed hard and hacked up black bile into her hand.

"Gross. Robin, will you grab me something to drink?"

Thea went to the sink and washed her hands of the bile. Healing people always took so much out of her, but at least she didn't pass out this time.
"Here, Lady." Robin handed her an icy glass of water. Thea gulped down the entire glass in one breath. "You did a great job," Robin said as she rubbed the small of Thea's back.

"Thank you for saving my wife!" Patrick was fighting back the tears as he hugged Ellie, and they were rocking side to side. Ellie ended the embrace and got up to run over to Thea and hugged her tight around her calf.
"Thank you! Thank you so much!" Ellie's small voice cried.

Thea smiled weakly at Ellie, bending down to hug her back. "You are so welcome, Ellie. I hope you are feeling better."

Thea's head started to pound behind her right eye. "Guys, I need to go lay down. Excuse me."

Thea stumbled as she walked over to the stairs to the loft. She staggered up the stairs with Fig in tow. "Thea? Do you need anything?" Robin asked.

Thea shook her head no as she slowly climbed the stairs. Ellie, Patrick, and Robin watched her with concern as she went up to her bed. Fig curled up around Thea's head and licked her little flyaway hairs as she drifted off to sleep.

When Thea awoke, it was the next day. Ellie had made a fruit basket from berries found in the surrounding forest and a beautiful bracelet full of sparkling gems and was a mass of silver that looked like twisted vines, holding the gems in place. Thea put on the bracelet and then remembered that gnomes are known for hoarding stolen jewelry. She felt uneasy wearing the extravagant bracelet and did not want to hurt Ellie's feelings if she happened to be downstairs.

Downstairs, Robin was sitting at the table and was slicing the arrowroot that was dried and then slowly grinding it into a powder.

"Hey, sleepyhead," Robin said with a smile.

"Hey." Thea's voice came out in a hoarse crackling noise. She cleared her throat. "Um, hey." She sat down and grabbed an apple and a glass of fizzy. "So, you have a house behind your stove?"

Robin smiled. "Doesn't everyone?"

Thea was curious as to what other secrets were hidden in plain sight around her friend's house.

Chapter Ten

Each day the girls would spend the mornings grinding the arrowroot into dust and making their pain potion; then, they spent the afternoons studying their books and working on Thea's defense abilities with her staff. This continued for a few weeks until they had enough bottles filled and labeled for sale.

"I suppose we should get ready to go to market," Robin stated as she boxed up the last of the bottles. "We are running low on food. I think we have roughly a hundred of these done. That should fetch us enough to get food through winter."

Thea stayed outside as long as she could –she and Fig were cuddled up under a big tree, reading her spellbook, with the rusty lock. As she flipped through the pages, she noticed that many had been ripped out of the back. The color of the paper, the texture was the same as the little notes that she had found along the way.

I guess I have been leaving myself notes. Thea thought. She held the book by its spine and shook it. A single strip of paper drifted out to the ground.

Ice can slow the heart that will not die. The words were scratched on it in the same ink and writing as the others. "Well, what do I mean by that?" Thea questioned the cat. Although she pondered, no answers readily came.

The next day the trio rose with the sun, and locked up Robin's cabin, started their trip to the market. Thea wore her cloak with the silver sparrow, with her bag tucked underneath, her staff in hand as her walking stick. Robin packed a small wagon with their fares. Fig settled down amongst the bottles and blankets for a nap. The trip was long and would take a couple of days.

"A horse. You need to get a horse, Robin." Thea said teasingly as she saw Robin struggling to pull her little wagon.

"Bugger off, Thea," Robin said under her breath with a smirk on her face.

They continued down the path, watching the birds chase each other in the trees. They were singing and skipping about when a little figure came running out onto the path from the bushes. It was an elf that was dressed all in green, with brown leather shoes. His ears were pointed, as was his nose. The elf tripped over his own feet, sending his cap flying into a mound of dirt, revealing a long scar across his forehead. Thea stopped in her tracks, startled at the little guy that was running in front of her.

"Is it you? The one that the fairies call Cannenta?" the little elf questioned. Thea tilted her head to the side and looked at the elf.

"You're that little elf that stabbed me when I was just trying to help you!" she yelled at the elf. The elf blushed as he was picking himself up off the ground, dusting off his knees.

"My apologies Miss. At the time, I thought that you were just a huge fairy, and I had no idea what you were doing to me. Please accept my..."

Thea was short, as she cut him off, "You're fine. Excuse us; we have someplace to be." She started to walk around him.

Robin looked at Thea awkwardly and followed in stride. Thea was still upset that the elf had stabbed her.

"Please wait! I am so sorry. I was sent to get you!" The elf scampered in front of Thea's path to try to stop her.

"By who?" Thea questioned with annoyance.

"My King is very sick and needs you." The elf was trying to keep up with Thea's stride and was struggling to catch his breath as he spoke.

"Does he like to stab people too?" Thea responded quite snarky.

"I thought you were one of those fairies. Again, fair lady, I apologize." The little elf stated with a solemn look on his face.

"Thea, we have to get going, or we are going to miss the market." Robin was getting annoyed by this whole situation as she struggled with the wagon of goods. "We REALLY don't have time for side trips."

"Please, ladies. We have been watching you practice your spells. I know now that you are not a fairy, but a….witch," the elf stammered out.

"I'm a healer." Thea responded, "Robin." That is all that she said in the direction of her friend. They made eye contact and stood there for a few seconds as if they were having a conversation without words. Robin's annoyance was clear on her face as she spoke.

"What are we going to do with this cart? You know we have to go far off the path to get to whoever he wants you to help. Do you know what's in the woods?" Robin was making large gestures with her arms as she pointed off into the dark of the forest.

"Excuse me," the little elf said as he tugged on Robin's skirt. "I will handle your cart, Miss."

With that, the little elf put his two pointer fingers into his mouth and whistled sweetly into the woods. There was a mighty squeal as a wild boar came running out of the forest towards the elf at full speed, and then turning on a dime, he slid sideways to stop quickly. Once the dust settled and the coughing had subsided, the little elf walked the boar over to Robin's cart. A brown leather harness was on the boar, tied around his tusks; the little elf attached the straps to the cart's handles.

"Doug will handle your cart. Please follow me," the elf said.

As they walked, the girls learned that the elf's name was Moonbeam, and he was a warrior for the Raven Kingdom of elves. Moonbeam rode on the back of Doug as the girls would have a horse.

"Moonbeam? Can you tell me why you and the fairies were fighting the last time we met?" Thea questioned the little elf.

Moonbeam turned his head to the side as he paused to listen. "Those creatures," he started with a smug tone to his voice, "Those fairies stole our land and our houses by the lake. We had lived by that lake for hundreds of years. The fairies put a sleeping spell on us and moved us to the middle of the forest where there are no lakes or brooks. They just moved us like we didn't matter."

The girls looked on to Moonbeam with a feeling of sorrow in their hearts.

"You see?" Robin questioned Thea in a whisper. "There are two sides to every story." Robin gave Thea a look with a raised eyebrow. The group continued in silence into the dense forest.

They walked for miles into the center of the darkest part of the woods where the sun barely shone through the trees, and the singing birds were far away. The grass was worn away, and the ground was covered with dust and moss. Doug trotted happily to a clearing in the trees and then stopped with a grunt and sat down on a pile of moss.

"We're here! I found her!" Moonbeam yelled.

There was a flurry of ravens flying down from the trees with little elves on their backs. There were hundreds of them circling around the girls and the small cat. All of the massive trees had lights going up to them that looked like apartment skyscrapers. The elves started to tug on Fig's ears and tail. With a mighty hiss, he leaped up onto Thea's shoulder, awkwardly trying to sit there as if he was a kitten and could balance there.

"Let him be!" Thea hissed down to the sea of green.

"Make room! We must see the king!" Moonbeam walked up to a giant tree and pounded on the door where a female elf in a flowing dress of sky blue and golden hair answered the banging.

"You're back!" she exclaimed as she wrapped her arms around Moonbeam.

"Starshine, this is Thea and Robin. They are the witches I told you about." He exclaimed proudly.

"Healer," Thea stated coldly.

"Well, get them into the house so we can save him.

He's fading fast!" Her grey eyes stared up at Thea with curiosity.
"I'm afraid I have to stab you one more time, Thea," Moonbeam said as he plunged an arrow into Thea's calf.

"Ow! You little..." Thea started to yell at the elf, but she quickly began to shrink smaller with each word that escaped her lips.

Soon, she was the same size as the little elves. She had fallen amongst her clothes, now standing there naked. The same had happened to Robin by a small arrow in her foot. They attempted to cover themselves in the folds of their clothes. Fig had his hair standing on end and was hissing at all the elves, batting at them with his paw, sending them flying.
"What are you doing?!" Thea and Robin were screaming at the elves. Starshine had run out of the house with dresses in hand.

"I hope these fit," she said sweetly as she reached out to offer the dresses to the naked girls. Thea shot an unsure glance at Robin.

"I told you I wanted to go to the market; this was your bright idea, mate," Robin said snidely as she snatched the dress out of Starshine's hand. The two dressed as quickly as they could. Thea went up to Moonbeam and grabbed him by the shirt collar.

"What did you do to me?" she yelled in his face.

"I have to get you into the house. You will go back to normal size soon, I promise." Thea pushed him down to the ground and walked over to the house. "I shouldn't even help you now! You could have just brought him to me, you idiot!" she yelled back to the elf as he was once again, dusting the knees of his pants and sulking with a bruised ego.

The girls walked into the small door of the tree to the fantastic palace of the elves. The floors glittered with gold tiling, and shining crystals lit the rooms. There were paintings of elf kings on the walls and elegant furniture.

"This way, please," Starshine gestured to the girls as she led them to the golden elevator lift that was being powered by a couple of field mice running on a track. It brought them to the top floor of the tree where there was the master suite. The Elf King, lying in his bed, was much older than the elves she had seen outside. He had white hair with a matching beard that was braided down his chest. His crescent glasses set on the tip of his pointed nose, and a sizeable bejeweled crown of gold upon his brow. He had a light sigh with each breath while he slept. Thea walked over to the Elf King and laid her hands on him as she had done with all the others heal. Nothing was happening—no electricity through her fingertips. There was no orb surrounding them, and there weren't sparks. Just the old man was softly sleeping.

"I'm sorry," Thea blushed. "It's not working." She turned to look at Moonbeam and softly shrugged her shoulders.

"You're not trying hard enough!" Moonbeam shrieked at her.

"You have to help him!" Starshine cried. Thea was wracking her brain on what she was doing wrong.

Robin leaned against the wall and folded her arms in front of her chest. "He's not injured or sick; he's just old. You can't heal someone being old." Thea looked solemnly at Robin and lightly nodded her head in agreeance.
"I'm sorry," is all Thea could say.

They made their way out of the tree as they started to grow back to their average size. They stood in the opening of their clothes, waiting for their bodies to fill in the voids of the fabric. They slowly filled out all of their clothes and grew back to the size that they originally were. The girls sat in the grass with their legs folded under them. The elves grumbled at the girls with disappointment and then left for their houses.

"What are we supposed to do without our king?"

"What can we do?" Thea asked Robin. Thea was flipping through her spell books, looking for an answer.

"I don't think there is anything we can do," Robin said as she lightly touched Thea's knee.

"There has to be something we can do," Thea whispered to herself. Fig stared into the windows of the palace as if he were watching his next meal.

"We should be going, Thea. I'm sure we're not as welcomed anymore, now that we can't help." Robin started to get the wagon ready to go and tried to rouse Doug from his nap.

"I've got it!" Thea exclaimed as she jumped up to grab her bag. "I found a spell that extends life!"

Thea pushed to book to Robin, and she skimmed the spell. The fairies used this spell to live for hundreds of years at a time.

"Where are you going to get fairy dust from? The elves and the fairies are at war over some land; the fairies won't help you," Robin stated as she tossed the book back to Thea.

A smile stretched across Thea's lips as she pulled the small bottle out of her bag that the Fairy Prince had given her. Robin took the bottle into her hand and looked at it in awe.

"You are always a surprise to me. What else do we need?" Robin looked at this as a game now and wanted to participate. The girls mixed a potion of fairy dust, dragonfly wings, lavender oil, honey, and venom of a scorpion into one of the elf's cooking pots. Moonbeam built a small fire and boiled the concoction until the steam turned orange and then blood red.

"Alright, Moonbeam, you need to get him to drink this. No more shrinking us!" She yelled as she saw him grab an arrow and start to come towards her.

Moonbeam took the brew to the king and forced his mouth open to drink. The girls watched through the small window as Starshine tilted the king's head back and held him as he started to cough. The coughs became violent, and the king shook vigorously as the brew made its way to his stomach. He coughed so hard; he ended up sitting up on his own. Then he opened his eyes and continued to cough for a few more moments. Moonbeam gave the king a drink from a bottle on the nightstand, and it calmed his body. Starshine and Moonbeam smiled back at the witches through the window with great excitement.

The sun had set, and the elves had started a celebration amongst the trees. The ravens were dropping flowers on the heads of the witches as they sat at the fire. A great feast was made, and they played music on their tiny flutes and drums and danced around the fire. The Elf King came to the window and watched the festivities; he was leaning on a cane, but it was the first time the king has been out of bed since they attacked the fairies.

The king opened the window and beckoned to the girls to come to talk to him. "Dear witches, thank you. I lost my son not long ago, and my daughter is not ready to lead the elves against the fairies. She wants to work with the fairies to share the land. You gave me time." He bowed his head to the girls.

"Your highness," Thea started. "I appreciate your concern for the fairies, but you should know that it was fairy dust that is allowing you to move around right now." The king seemed shocked and then disgusted. "As a friend keeps reminding me: there are two sides to every story," She said with a mocking tone to her voice, as she looked at Robin.

The girls slept under Thea's fairy blanket in the moss

surrounding the elven camp. Fig was waiting to pounce on the elves that were walking by, heading to their houses. "Don't do it, cat." Robin boxed Fig's ears.

"Do you think we did the right thing?" Thea asked Robin sleepily.

"Well, if we didn't, it's too late now," Robin said with a yawn showing her typical indifference.

The girls cuddled up by the dying embers of the fire and watched the few stars they could see through the trees. Just as they were drifting off to sleep, a crow cawed sharply in the distance. Thea shook herself awake and got wide-eyed as she stared off into the dark of the forest. The ravens in the trees looked down at the girls and then took off in a murder towards the calling crow. Her pounding migraine was back again. She pulled out a bottle of their arrowroot tonic and had a swig of the sweet water. Thea smiled and settled back into her little bed of moss. She felt safe with the ravens watching over her. She looked up to see where her little cat had settled for the night and saw Fig was cuddled up with Doug at the foot of the fire; the cat was slowly licking the head of the wild boar. Thea smiled and wondered how long that friendship would last or if Fig was planning his breakfast.

Chapter Eleven

When the girls woke the next morning, they had gifts waiting for them from the elves. There were baked cookies and bread wrapped in small cloths, wild purple carrots, and yams in sacks that the elves had stacked into the wagon. The village women had added to the decoration on Thea's cloak; they have embroidered a raven next to the sparrow. Thea smiled at Starshine. "You see, maybe sparrows and ravens can live together," she whispered to the tiny elf.

Moonshine walked up to the girls and handed each of them a small jar with an emerald liquid inside.

"This is what was on the arrows that made you shrink down to our size," he said. "Be careful. You only need a few drops to do it. It lasts for about an hour, and then you will grow back to your original size. It only works on humans, though. Don't let your cat get into it." He smiled a devilish smile at the cat who had been trying to eat him since they met.

Moonshine had offered Doug's services back to the road. The girls packed the rest of their items and started. "You know, your bottle collection for spells is going to be amazing if you keep helping all of these creatures," Robin said with a smirk as they dug their walking sticks into the dirt. Fig was sitting on Doug's back as the group made their way back to the dirt path. The ravens were flying overhead, following them and watching their every move.

"I think this is more useful than any bottle I get," Thea said as she pointed to her feathered friends flying overhead.

They made it to the dirt road and let Doug off of the harness of the wagon. Fig went over, and the two nuzzled their heads together, saying their good-byes.

"Thank you, Doug," Robin said as she scratched under his tusk. With a grunt, the wild boar turned on his hoofs and was back into the thicket of the forest.

Through the sunflower field, they continued to the market with their raven protectors flying overhead over the tiny houses. They made it to the booth right before the sunset. The trio made camp in the booth for the evening. A raven perched on each of the four corners of the tiny booth. Robin had pulled out some fabric from the bottom of the wagon and tied them from post to post of the booth to make themselves hammocks for the evening. Fig had settled in his usual spot on the oversized chair.

"This is like old times. Not that you remember it, but we use to camp in here once a month when we would do a big haul of product. It is sort of the middle point between our houses." Robin said as she jumped into one of the hammocks, making the whole booth sway. She kicked her shoes off and had her stripped stocking foot hanging over the side. Thea walked around, tightened all the flaps of her booth, then unloaded the wagon onto the shelves before climbing into her hammock.

Morning came, and the witches were awakened by the other merchants' clatter setting up their booths. The girls took down their beds and split some of the berries and bread they had left in their stash. They opened up their booth to see Eleonore's smiling face across the way, setting up her own booth.

"Dearie! Good morning my dear!" Her sweet voice carried across the walkway.

"Good morning Eleonore!" the girls waved to her. Thea walked over and traded a bottle of their tonic for a few loafs of cardamom bread.

It didn't take long for the marketplace to be buzzing with

people looking for a deal, merchants peddling their wares. Thea looked up to see her raven bodyguards still hanging out above their booth. She walked down the way and purchased meats, cheeses, preserve, and dried fruits. She bought a new barrette to give to Robin to tame down her wild hair. When she walked back to the booth, Robin was busy pushing the arrowroot tonic to heal pretty much any ailment that people had.

"Oh, sure! It can help with that too." Robin said to a man with a bandage on his shoulder.

"What happened to you?" Thea questioned the man.

"Ah, I got hit with an arrow. Hunting accident." He said with shifting eyes and hesitation.

"Here," Thea said as she handed the man a different bottle with thyme inside. "Grind it up and mix a little water with it to make a paste. Put it directly on the wound. It will help it heal and numb the pain on the outside. The tonic water will help with the pain internally." Thea said with a smile. The man nodded at her and gave Robin a small bag full of coins.
"What's this?" Thea questioned as she picked up a small wooden box off the counter.

"I'm not sure; where did that come from?" Robin responded with a perplexed look.

Thea examined the box in front of her face. It was hand-painted blue with golden inlays swirled across the wood.

"It was sitting here," Thea responded as she gestured to the spot on the counter.

"What's inside?" Robin asked as she looked around to see if anyone else on the street was paying attention to what they were doing.

"I guess there is only one way to find out," Thea said as she opened the box's latch. A small piece of confetti floated out of the box with a sweet smell of baked cookies. It floated up to the center of the walkway and started to expand in the air. People began to gather around and had their noses in the air. The wafting smell of cookies had attracted the majority of the market. Even Fig had gotten off his chair and was on the counter watching the show. The small paper started to blow up like a balloon and was the size of Thea's head. Bright colors of yellow and pink illuminated from the gadget as it spun. Ravens started to squawk at the balloon as it now was growing larger, music began to play from the balloon-like a carousel. People began to clap along with the music, and the children were dancing around.

Thea looked nervously at Robin, who was fascinated with the spectacle. A face appeared in the middle of the balloon of a beautiful maiden; she was laughing and smiling with the music. Her skin had a blue hue that extended out to the tips of her hair. The balloon was almost as tall as a small child at this point. It started to spin in a circle, keeping in time with the music playing from within. As it turned faster and faster, the music's tempo increased until it started to miss notes. The people stopped their clapping and dancing to look at the balloon and see what would happen next. The face in the balloon was no longer smiling. Her face had twisted to a face filled with excruciating pain. She was screaming and yelling within the balloon. The smell of sweet cookies in the air was no longer there, replaced with the scent of a dead skunk started from the balloon. Black smoke began to follow as the balloon was now the same size as Thea.

"Run," Robin whispered from her lips. "Run!" she screamed louder at the group of people.

They were stupefied in their spots. Robin reached over the counter and grabbed their staff, tossing one at Thea, who caught it out of the air. The balloon's smoke took over the air of the marketplace. The ravens were diving at the balloon and dropping rocks onto it. Fig was standing on the counter, ready to pounce. His deep throaty growl echoed. The face in the spinning balloon went from screaming to hysterically laughing. The balloon swelled, and the smoke was filling their lungs, causing them to cough and hack for air. The size of the balloon could not stretch any farther. "BOOM!" It exploded with a force that knocked people over. The laughing head was now audible and was attached to a body.

The people who were dancing about were now lying on the ground, gasping for breath, coughing in the thick, black smoke. Thea had her staff out, ready to attack. Robin was leaning against the booth with a scarf wrapped around her face. Thea recognized the woman that was standing in front of her. It was the caramel-skinned woman who had visited her the last time she was at the market. The Crow Witch was sitting where the balloon had once been and laughed with her head held back. The ravens were still swooping at her with their rocks in their beaks. One of their stones made a direct hit with her eye, and her laughter stopped. She started to swat at the incoming attacks – the black smoke began to billow off, and people were able to breathe. The Crow Witch started to focus her attention on Thea.

"Do I have your attention now?" the Crow Witch asked.
She lifted her arms above her head, and lightning started to come in from the sky as thunderbolts filled her hands. "We've been looking for you, Thea!" she shouted as she shot a bolt at Thea's feet.

Thea rolled out of the way of the attack. Robin lunged forward at the Crow Witch, and her staff made contact with her ribs and then the side of her temple. A thunderbolt that the witch had in her hand went rouge, connecting to the side of a booth down the way. Splinters of wood shattered through the air and impaled some of the spectators. The Crow Witch fell onto her side with a grunt. Thea attacked her from the other side.

"I don't know what you want from me!" Thea yelled at the witch as she, too, connected her staff with the witch's head. "But you are not going to hurt these people!"

The witch got to her feet from a squatting position and then lunged onto Thea's back – digging her nails into Thea's skin around her collarbone, bringing them down to a scuffle on the ground.

"I need you alive for Lilly!" the witch yelled.

People were running and screaming as the booth that had caught the thunderbolt was now flaming wildly. The stalls' wooden covers were slamming shut as people hid with their children– peering out to watch the commotion still happening.

Thea was bleeding and had the Crow Witch still fighting with her from her back. Robin was screaming at the witch as she was beating on her back with her staff. The Crow Witch removed one hand from fighting with Thea and made a swooping motion towards Robin. Robin's staff went flying to the left, and Robin's body went flying to the right. Fig had leaped off the counter and sunk his teeth into the Crow Witch's neck. She squealed in pain as she grabbed the little cat from the scruff of his neck and sent him flying back into the booth. Thea was grasping at the witch's hands that were now wrapped around Thea's neck, crushing her trachea. Robin got to her feet, and her rage was showing through her eyes. Her fiery hair was standing on end, and she had her hands out to the sides of her hips facing out towards the ground. The dirt and the mud started to rumble and rise along with her.

"Fight with me!" she commanded as small mud trolls started to form and attack the Crow Witch.

She released her grip from Thea's neck, and the smoky air started to fill Thea's lungs with a gasp. She backed up and got to her feet. She grabbed her staff and swung it at the Crow Witch. She felt the surge of power run through her arms and out the staff's tip shooting a massive fireball towards the witch. The flame struck her in the face and knocked her backward over her heels. She screamed in pain as the smell of burning flesh filled Thea's nostrils while jabbing her staff into the stomach of the witch. The mud trolls, one by one, started to jump on top of the Crow Witch, pinning her to the ground while the murder of ravens tripled in size, swooping upon her body. They attacked her burning flesh and ripped her eyes out of their sockets. The Crow Witch's scream was so loud and high pitched that it shattered everything glass in the market place. Another black puff of smoke appeared. The witch transformed into a crow, crashing into the tops of the booths before flying off toward the forest's dark area with the group of ravens in pursuit. Silence filled the streets of the market. The people were all peeking out of the booths in fear as they stared at the two girls. Their chests were heaving – they were bloody, bruised, and covered in soot and dirt.

"Who was that?" Thea panted out to Robin.

Robin picked up her staff and limped over to where Thea was sitting in the street's dirt and offered her a hand up.

"That was Thalia. Lilly Quinn's youngest cousin. I don't know what you did to that coven, but they want you dead."

The girls looked over the street at the terrified faces of the people. The amount of destruction that was left behind was beyond measure.

"You…. you're a witch," Eleonore stammered out from behind her booth with one finger pointing directly at Thea. "Stay away from me!" Eleonore screamed.

Chapter Twelve

"Here, let me help you," Thea said as she approached one of the people who got hit by the exploding booth.

"Stay away from me! Haven't you done enough? You witch!" Thea was taken aback by the response that she was getting from the people she was trying to help.

The group looked on with fear as the two witches walked through the market. "We're the same people we were before.

"We did not do this!" Thea yelled at the people who were running from them.

Robin did not seem phased by the way people were reacting to them.

"See? People like you until you get labeled as a witch. When you were just Thea, the healer, you were just fine to be around." Robin was talking softly but angrily next to Thea as they walked over to the broken booth.

A few people were trying to pick others up off the ground. Thea trotted over to them. "Please, let me heal you," the man who had the arrow wound was amongst the group that got hit. He allowed Thea to touch him. She put her hands on the piece of wood that was sticking out of his stomach, then pulled until she fell backward with the large splinter of wood in her hands. She then placed the palm of her hand over his wound. As she shut her eyes, her hair had the static charge of the electrical current that flowed through her body and into the man.

"Would you look at that?" She heard the people watching comment as the man's wound slowly closed up and turned into a fresh scar.

She did the same to the arrow wound on his shoulder. "Thank you, Thea." He stated to her as he slowly rose. His rugged features soften as he looked into her eyes. Thea weakly smiled back at him; then she started to cough up the black bile that seemed to infect her whenever she healed someone. Once the people of the market saw that she was not hurting anyone, they lined up to have their shrapnel removed, and their skin healed. Robin passed out small bottles of their arrowroot tonic to help with the internal pain.

The girls assisted with cleaning up the broken booths and paid the rugged man to rebuild them. That's all they could do. By the time Thea got back to her end of the market, Eleonore had packed up and left. Thea's heart felt heavy as she realized that her friend did not want anything to do with her anymore. The girls packed up their booth and settled in for the night. Thea was finally able to tend to Robin's ailments as well.

"Too bad you can't heal yourself," she said to Thea.

Thea's body was getting stiff as she plopped down in the overstuffed chair with Fig. "That would be amazing right now," Thea said as she rubbed lavender oil on her temple.

"Well, it's a good thing that we made so many of these," she said as she tossed an arrowroot bottle to Thea. Thea sipped on the little bottle as she stared off down the road, watching everyone pack up to head home for the day.

"You said Thalia is part of a coven, right?" Thea asked Robin.

"That's right. She's related to Lilly Quinn." Thea still hasn't lifted her gaze from the road.

"Where do they camp?" Thea continued; her expression had hardened as she slowly stroked Fig's soft fur. Robin perked up from her hammock.

"You saw how beat up we got from one witch, and you want to go hunt down a coven?" Robin laughed and rolled her eyes.

"Well, they seem to be looking for me. If I know where they camp, I can either avoid it to save my life or go hunt them all down, to save my life." Thea stated.

Robin pointed to the south of town. "They have a town to the south called Edgehaven."

Thea nodded as she listened. "See? Now I know and can make my own choice. Life is about choices." Thea stated.

The girls heard the calls of the ravens as they had made it back to the market. They were playing catch with Thalia's eyeball, tossing it from post to post. "I don't see any good that could possibly come from that," Thea said as she started to braid her hair.

"At least you can see," Robin said with an amused smirk as she watched the raven's game. Thea caught a case of the giggles and couldn't help but laugh at Robin's lame pun. "That's not funny," she tried to say with a straight face.

"Can I have that please?" Thea said to the ravens with her hand out. A large raven with blue-tipped wings hesitantly dropped it into Thea's palm. "Thank you, sweet friend." She said as she dropped the eye into a bottle and filled it with some liquid.

"You ruined their fun," Robin said as she tossed one of Fig's cat toys up in the air for the ravens.

The witches kept their booth closed the next morning as Thea was still resting from their adventure the day before. She finally stopped coughing up, bile around two in the morning, and got some rest. She rubbed thyme on her wounds and changed the dressing on them. Bruises over her collarbones matched that of Thalia's hands perfectly. The girls stayed quiet most of the day, listening to the people outside who were gossiping about the Crow Witch. By the day's end, her' tale of the Crow Witch' was larger than a giant, and her were fireballs hotter than Hades. Thea just shook her head as she read her books in the overstuffed chair and drifted in and out of sleep.

"Tomorrow, I am going to head back to my cabin," Thea decided. "You are more than welcomed to join me if you'd like. I feel that there is something that I am missing from there that will tell me what happened between me and this sisterhood." Thea was turning her pendant between her fingers as she read her spellbook.

"That sounds like a plan to me," Robin said excitedly as she swung back and forth in her hammock.

"Hey. How did you make those mud trolls?" Thea asked without looking up from her book.

"Huh? Oh, I do it the same way you make fireballs. You have a fire element, and I have an earth."

Thea sat and contemplated that for a moment.

"So, the Crow Witch has air?" Thea responded, now looking up from her book.

"Hmmm, I would guess so since she can make thunderbolts. Only a supreme witch will have more than one element within her. My mom had three, but she never was able to do fire. So close to being a supreme." Robin said as she got a little teary-eyed talking about her mom.

Thea gave her a half-smile and reached up and grabbed her foot. "There, there, little bear," she said as she stuck her tongue out.

"Nerd," Robin responded as she wiped her face with her sleeves.

The girls started early the next day. Thea took everything they could carry in the wagon with them and cleaned out the shelves. After what she witnessed with the Crow Witch, she seriously doubted that anyone would be buying anything from the booth any time soon. She shook Fig from his slumber. "Come on, Fig, lead us home."

He meowed in protest but got up, stretched, butt in the air, then started to trot down the market to the path leading towards Thea's small cabin. They passed Eleonore and Flynn's farm, which was in much better shape than the last time Thea had seen it. The fences and the walls were all mended with a fresh coat of paint on the barn. She saw that all the horses and cows had made it home as well. She wanted to stop but knew that Eleonore didn't want to see her. The girls left a bottle of tonic on the fence for Flynn. Thea sighed as they continued down the dirt path to the open field.

Deer were jumping through the long grass; a few had fawn following behind them. The sun was heading towards the west, and Thea knew that she wouldn't make it all the way home before night fall.

"We better find a place to camp," Thea said as they entered back into the wooded area of the path.

Robin was humming as she pulled the cart. "Are you sure? We're kind of out in the open out here." Robin responded as she looked around.

"Well, when the sun goes down, we lose the path," Thea stated as she stopped and turned to face Robin.

"Fair enough. I'm hungry anyway."

They went into the thicket about one hundred feet and set up their camp. Thea started a fire, except this time she used just her hand instead of smacking rocks together.

"This is much easier to do than what I was doing before," Thea said with a chuckle.

Robin smiled and pulled out a skillet she had bought at the market.
"Whoa! Nice," Thea gestured to Robin's new skillet.

"We made a lot of money before that witch showed up." Robin jingled her coin pouch and danced to the rhythmic clanking of the coins with a smile. Robin made them grilled cheese with a side of bacon that they had bought.

"Good thing Doug isn't here anymore." Thea joked as she devoured her dinner. Thea was doing her best to study the elements from her books by the campfire but failed to focus or to see the words on the page.

"How do you figure out what elements you have?" Thea questioned Robin, who was trying to get her hammock set up between two trees.

"Well, you know how you focus all of your emotion and energy into the pit of your stomach, and then you open your palm and focus it there?" Thea nodded in response.

"Well, you need to do that but try to focus on the other elements that you want to use. I almost got fire once." Robin said as she finally looked over to Thea. "But it just came out as black smoke and singed my eyebrows. Still pretty scary, though." Robin said as she rubbed her brows in remembrance.

Thea smirked at her. She stood and focused all of her emotion into the pit of her stomach and concentrated. She thought about her fight with the Crow Witch and started to feel hot within her core. Then she turned her palms up to the sky and tried to focus on the air. She imagined she was pulling all of the air from the atmosphere into her hand as if a tornado was spinning down to her. The clouds started to form above the trees, and Thea shook as if she was having a seizure. There was a loud crack of thunder, and then a thunderbolt fell right in front of her, hitting the fire pit. The wood crackled, and sparks were flying in all directions. Fig dove and took cover behind a boulder, and Robin spun around and grabbed her staff, not knowing Thea was practicing a spell. The second thunderbolt that hit the ground lit up the entire forest. Thea dropped her hands to her side; she could hear the animals and creatures scattering out in the darkness.

"Well, so much for not letting anyone know we're here," Robin said as she grabbed her heart. "A little warning next time?"

Robin and Thea settled into the hammocks, and Fig had jumped up onto Thea's stomach. The wind was gently rocking the hammocks, and the crickets had finally started to sing again after the thunder that Thea had conjured up.

"I think you are onto it, Thea." Robin started. "That was a good first try. You may want to find a lake or a stream, though, to do the water. It's a little softer to practice with." Robin yawned.

"How many supremes are there?" Thea questioned. "Like is there a bunch, or just a few? And how do you know? Do you just stumble upon your elements?" Thea's mind was racing as she was trying to figure out what she could do.

"Usually, when you are a young girl, the elements let you know. I always moved rocks that would be much too heavy for someone my size to move. You, I remember, could light candlesticks by transferring fire with a swift movement of your fingers."

Thea was rocking back and forth in her hammock. "Just like everything in life, it has two sides to it. One side of your element can do well; on the other, you can hurt yourself. There have been witches who have drowned or burned themselves. I almost buried myself alive....oh and electrocuting themselves with thunderbolts," she ended with a chuckle.

"Hey, I'm sorry. I thought it would turn out to be an orb-like when I do the fire." Thea said in a teasing tone back.

She started playing with the pendant around her neck as she was thinking about how she may control the elements. "Those mud trolls are brilliant. I want to learn how to do that." Thea said to Robin.

"I'm sure you can, Thea. You have always been more talented than me. Your fire is the strongest element, though." Thea thought about what Robin said.

"Yeah, but I'd rather restrain someone with some mud trolls instead of burning their face-off. I can't believe what I did to her face." Thea said with a shudder.

"She got what she had coming to her. She attacked us first!" Robin was getting into her emotions again.

"Calm down!" Thea said teasingly. "You're going to conjure up some creatures again."

The girls talked and giggled until the wee hours of the morning when they drifted off to sleep as the wind rocked them back and forth.

There was a faint jingle in the air; a high pitched chime, getting louder and louder. Thea stirred in her sleep. Something was tickling her nose, and she swatted at it.

"Meow!" Fig cried as he pounced, landing on Thea's face. "What the hell, cat?!" Thea screeched.

"Wake up, Human!" Thea couldn't focus on the hot pink orb that was circling her head. "Human!" the small voice screamed in Thea's face.

"Willow? What are you doing here?" Robin was now up and had a few hundred fairies pointing their poison-tipped arrows at her face.

"Uh, Thea? Friends of yours?" Robin questioned as she stared back at the little fairies with wide eyes.

"Willow, what is going on? Let my friend go," Thea demanded. With a nod, the fairies dispersed from Robin's face.

"We need your help, Human! The elves are back, and they brought the nymphs with them!" Thea stood up from her bed.

"The name is Thea," she corrected the fairy as she sat scratching her head and looking over to Robin.

"Willow, the elves and others have said that this was their land first and that you tricked them out of it. Is that true?"

Willow's jaw dropped for just a second as she looked over her shoulder at Thea. Then Willow squinted her eyes tight as she turned around to face the witches. "I don't think the elves would tell you the truth when they were defeated. History is only told by those who have won the war," Willow stated coldly.

"I'm not sure if that answers what I asked you," Thea replied.

"She's a flipping fairy, Thea! You can't believe anything that comes out of her mouth. They see humans as playthings, not as someone to respect." Robin was aggravated and caught a small arrow into her arm for speaking her mind.

"Do as you want, Human. Just remember: the blood of the fallen will be because YOU didn't come when your help was asked for." Willow made a rude gesture at Robin before she whistled, and the few hundred fairies flew off towards their fairy circle that Thea had visited before.

Thea looked in the direction that the fairies retreated. The girls could see explosions of bright light bursting a few miles in the darkness. They could hear the cries of the ravens from where they stood.

"We have to stop them from murdering each other," Thea said to Robin.

The look on Robin's face was of pure annoyance. "I already knew you were going to say that." The girls collected their things and smothered out the fire. They heard a twig snap off in the distance, the opposite way of the fairy circle. All that could be seen were shadows. Fig, with his hair on end, hissed in the darkness.

"Fight the unknown, or fight the little creatures who are fighting each other?"

Chapter Thirteen

They each picked up their staffs and pulled their wagon towards the war ahead. The noise ahead sounded like fireworks as they neared the battle. The tree elves that the girls had helped just a few days before were attacking the fairies, but this time, they brought reinforcements. The Water Nymphs stood five feet tall and had human forms in all aspects, except for their hypnotic beauty, which took away the breath of all who looked upon them, with hair that flowed as if they were still under water, in the shade of seafoam blue and skin that glowed, even in the moonlight. The Nymphs were off to the side of the battle; launching water bombs at the fairies, causing their wings to become wet, making them unable to fly. Ravens were there, assisting the elves and chasing the much smaller sparrows back into the trees. Bright colors were exploding throughout the night sky in bursts of pink and blue as spells were shot across the trees.

"This is utter chaos," Robin whispered as they watched from a distance away.

"What happens when they kill each other?" Thea questioned. "You heard the fairy. The victor is the one who writes the history. I want to know what is so special about this land," Robin responded.

They crept in the shadows as they moved towards the fairy circle. Colorful orbs were flying every which way and the birds were diving at each other. Bombs and poisoned arrows were zinging past their heads, and the ground was littered with tiny bodies. They all were dressed for battle, as if they knew this was going to be happening this night. Armored bodies on the back of birds were flying through the trees. The elves wore armor that was painted with the same raven figure that was on Thea's cloak, and the fairies had the sparrow embroidered in rich colors across their capes. Swords and bows drawn, there was no hesitation in the attack.

"Stop!" Thea yelled as she started to swat at the airborne attacks. "This doesn't need to happen!" she screamed. She was now in the middle of the battle field. She pulled a small poisoned dart out of her neck and felt woozy. "Robin, have your trolls clear the ground!"

Robin stood next to Thea and the ground started to shake as the tiny trolls started to rumble out of the dirt. One by one her creatures started to pick up the fallen and moved them to the base of one of the trees; a pile of fairies and a pile of elves. The numbers of injured totaled into the thousands.

Thea was doing her best to separate the two groups and was failing horribly. That's when she saw him; the Elf King! He was riding on the largest of the ravens – soaring up to the palace window of Queen Anastasia with a bomb lit in his hand. He threw it into her window, sending shards of glass flying into the palace. Just before the branch of the tree exploded, a light pink fairy came flying out of the window at great speed.

Thea needed to do something to gain their attention. She stood in the middle of the fairy circle and conjured a fireball in her hand that she threw up into the sky. Only a few of the birds were bothered by her fireball attempt and left the scene. Everyone else continued to fight. Robin had the water nymphs restrained with her mud trolls and Fig had the wounded separated, but there was no way for them to reach the air attacks above their heads.

"Thunderbolt!" Robin yelled over to Thea.

She hesitated, as the last time she did that she almost killed herself. She took that fear and focused her hands up to the sky, shaking. The sky illuminated with such a bright light that it no longer looked to be night. The electricity poured down into her hands and she dropped to one knee as she threw the thunderbolt to the ground. The fireworks had stopped as the birds and fairies were running from the battle field to find shelter. More thunderbolts came crashing down to the ground around Thea. She shrieked with each one that hit the ground like flashes of falling stars kissing the earth. The sky opened up and the rain started to pour down while the electricity from the thunderbolts were still dancing across the ground. The mud trolls turned back to mud puddles, and the only creatures that seemed to enjoy the rain were the nymphs who now were able to retreat back to the lake. Thea looked up to the sky and embraced the icy drops upon her face. The battle field was being cleansed by the rain, all that could be heard was the rain meeting the earth's mud puddles.

The rain slowly puttered to a stop, and there was silence in the forest once again. The two witches stood in the center of the fairy circle looking at the destruction of the forest. Water dripping from their clothes and they shivered in the wind. Thea conjured a fireball that she placed into a bush for light. There were too many fallen to count who had won this battle.

"Do you see what damage your behavior causes?!" Thea yelled out to the darkness. "Do you see what you are doing to your peoples? Your families? For what?" She slowly spun in a circle and yelled out to the creatures she knew were watching from the thicket of the forest, but none were brave enough to respond.

Robin helped Thea line up the little bodies as she tried to heal as many as she could. She was weak, tired, and wet. Robin passed out arrowroot dust to them and shook some of the fairy dust onto the fallen. There were too many to save and not enough power left in Thea. She started to bawl as she placed her hand on what seemed to be the thousandth small body and pushed her power into it. Thea was coughing up bile and finally fell over in a slump and was unresponsive for a moment. Robin ran to her side and picked her up out of the mud. She grabbed one of the fairies and shook her dust over Thea.

"Are you all happy now? She can't handle fixing everything that you break!" Robin hissed at the creatures who were peeking out from their houses and the surrounding forest. Robin laid Thea by the edge of the fire. She looked up to see Anastasia looking down from her palace window and shook her head in disgust up at the Fairy Queen.

"She needs to wake up!" Willow came zipping by Robin's head. "There are so many injured that need her help!"

Robin reached up and grabbed Willow by her leg and swung her around to face her. "You all made this choice to fight," she started out sternly in a low voice. "We were asleep, and you came and decided to involve us." Robin's voice started to become angrier and louder with each word. "This is not my fight!" she screamed at the little fairy. Robin flung Willow across the circle into a tree, as she screamed "Leave us alone! She needs to live! I need her to live!"

Robin started to slap Thea's face and Fig was licking her hand. "Come on! Wake up Thea!" She finally hit Thea hard enough that she opened her eyes and started to hack and cough. She rolled over onto her side and discarded a pile of the blackest bile she had yet produced.

"Water," is all Thea could rasp.

One of the elves came over with a canteen of water. She drank its entire contents in one gulp.

"How many more do I need to help?" Thea asked weakly.
"None, Thea. They did this to themselves and I am not going to sit by and watch you kill yourself because of these creatures." Robin was petting Thea's hair back away from her

face, and speaking to her in a soft, soothing voice, the way a mother would to her sick child. "You need to rest now."

Thea attempted to fight the forced restraint, and then realized that she could not handle healing one more body. "Call a parlay," Thea said in a small voice. "Get the Elf King and Anastasia. Call a parlay." With that last word Thea lost consciousness again. She fell into a deep, dreamless sleep.

Thea did not wake until nine days later in a small cave down by the lake. There was the sweet smell of burning leaves blowing through the cavern. The creatures had left her a jug with water and some dried meat next to her blanket. Fig's sweet face was nuzzling her cheek.

"I'm awake, Fig," she said with a moan. She could feel her heart beat behind her right eye and the warmth of a fire on her cheek. She slowly opened her eyes and saw Fig just a few inches away from her nose, watching her intently.

Robin walked into the opening of the cave not long after Thea woke up. "You better drink some water. I'm sure you are quite dehydrated." Robin unloaded more food out of her bag onto the blanket and joined her friend for brunch. "You have left an impression on both ends. They agreed to a standoff, until you woke up for your 'parlay'," Robin made air quotes as she talked in a sarcastic tone.

"I take it you still feel we should not interfere with these creatures and their fight?" Thea questioned.

Robin nodded in agreeance as she was slicing pieces of an apple and eating them off the blade of the knife. "Not my fight," Robin said sternly.

"But what happens when they destroy each other? Where is the balance of the universe then?" Robin just looked back at her stubbornly as Thea continued. "We're all here for a reason…fairies, elves, humans, cats, everything….if we allow them to kill each other off, then where is the balance?"

They sat there in silence for a few moments. Robin slowly chewing her breakfast and watching her friend get situated against the wall of the cave.

"I think you hit your head when you passed out," Robin said jokingly as she tossed a crust of bread at her.

Thea stuck her tongue out at Robin. "I'm serious."

The girls finished their brunch and then Robin left to get the Elf King and Anastasia. They were joined by the little blue fairy and Moonbeam. There was also a water nymph in tow who wore a silvery crown wrapped around her forehead, with her silvery blue hair wrapped amongst it into a messy bun.

"Thank you for the parlay." Thea started as she sipped on some sweet tea. "We need to find a better way for you all to settle this battle." The elves and the fairies glared at each other and the nymph sat with the straightest, stiff posture off to the side. "You cannot kill each other. You need to find a compromise that won't hurt one another." Thea continued on calmly.

"The land belongs to the fairies. When the elves stole our gold, we earned the right to the land," Anastasia hissed furiously. Moonbeam was the first to respond. "We did not steal your gold! You kidnaped us in our sleep!" He was on his feet with his hand reaching for his dagger.

"You also stopped the water flowing through our dam." The nymph softly interjected without showing any emotions.

"You stole their gold?" Thea questioned with her eyebrow

raised.

"We FOUND gold." The Elf King stated with an emphasis on the word found. "There was no reasoning for us to think that it would be their gold."

Thea let out a sigh. "And you put a dam in to stop water from filling the nymph's lake?" she directed towards the fairies.
"We didn't do that." Willow snapped from the entrance of the cave. Thea could feel the pain starting back up in her head. Perhaps she shouldn't have started such a difficult mediation so quickly after reawakening. She was far too irritable to be a calm, fair mediator.

"I don't think anyone is going to take responsibility for anything that has happened to the others, but regardless, killing each other is not the answer to solving it." Thea was rubbing her temple as she sat and with her legs crossed. "What if you both live here? There are plenty of trees around the lake. Besides, you have blown up so much of the fairy circle, you will need to move it anyway."

All of the creatures started to speak at once and the noise was too high pitched for Thea or Robin to make any sense of what was being said. Chaos ensued.

"I will not be living with these creatures!" The Elf King yelled as he drew his sword and pointed it at the fairies.

Willow flew over with her dagger drawn towards the Elf King; Fig swatted her down and she fell from the air with a thud against the cavern wall.

"Stop!" Thea yelled as she grabbed the Elf King and pushed the fairies away with her other hand.

"Father! It does not have to be like this!" Starshine had

followed Willow into the cave.

"We do not need to kill or steal to live," Starshine stated in a calm voice that could barely be heard over the clamor of the still rattled group.

Thea smiled at Starshine. "Exactly." Thea finally found an ally. The nymph sat there watching the chaos with an indifferent look on her face.

"You each lost more than a thousand bodies," Thea grunted as she was almost laying on the ground to separate the two groups. "I will not be helping either of you with your fallen!" Thea started to yell at the two groups who were getting ready to attack one and other once again.

The nymph stood up and walked towards the entrance. She paused at the door and looked over her shoulder at the group and stated in an icy voice: "Leave my lake and my Nymphs alone." She then gracefully glided out of the cave and continued into the lake until her head was completely submerged by the calm water.

"Well, there is one group done," Robin said with an unhelpful eye roll as she had now settled herself against the wall with her forearms resting on her bent knees.

"There is enough land on either side of this lake. You will still be by the water, and you will each have a side. The land you were fighting over is destroyed anyway, so even if you had won the land you would still need to move." Thea was now talking in a very calm and soothing voice. "We will set up the border lines of the lake. Elves will live on the East and fairies will live on the West. You will leave the water flow of the lake alone, as well as, the Nymphs."

Starshine was watching on and smiled with the words that

Thea said. Robin was giggling to herself as she watched.

"We will not live by someone who steals from us." This was the first time that Anastasia had contributed to the conversation.

"You both are in the wrong! This is not going to be solved by you two fighting over who is right. Figure it out." Thea let go of the two groups and walked over to the entrance of the cave with a stagger to her step. "I'm going to build a border for you two. You're both idiots and I wish you luck. May you figure it out." Thea left the cave with Fig and Robin in tow.

"See? I told you that this wasn't our fight. These groups have been fighting for longer than humans have been alive and will continue to do so afterwards."

Thea had a heavy heart. "It doesn't matter where it started. They both think they are in the right. The only one who gets it is Starshine, and by saving her father we stopped her from being in power. There may have been peace without us helping." Thea was shaking her head. "I just don't understand."

The girls collected branches and lined them up the beach of both sides of the lake; creating a makeshift fence that created the border. The fairies and elves were watching in their own groups. Starshine walked over to where the fairies were flying and offered a flower to Anastasia. No words were spoken, but she laid the flower on the ground, and nodding at the Fairy Queen, before retreating to her group. "Did you see that, Robin? That's hope." Thea said with a smile as they were walking to the north beach. The nymphs poked their heads out of the lake, just high enough for their eyes to be seen over the top of the water, watching all the groups of creatures on the shore. When eye contact was made, they dropped back into the depths.

"Let's get to the cabin. I did all I can do with these creatures." The three started back to the dirt road and slowly made their way towards Thea's home.

Chapter Fourteen

"You know they're going to start fighting again, right?" Robin said as she pulled the wagon.

"You really need to make up your mind. Do you want me to be involved, or is this not our fight?" Thea snapped at her.

"The world needs people like you. People that care." That was the best that Robin could come up with as a response.

"So, why don't you care?" she questioned Robin. The two continued down the road with their little cat friend, watching the debate from the back of the wagon.

"No one cared when I've had fights before. You have to learn that it is easier if you just mind your business. It's not my fight and doesn't affect me." Robin shrugged her shoulders indifferently, but how she stared ahead down the road suggested more emotion behind the words than she let on.

Thea was silent for a second. "That's the dumbest thing I have ever heard. I have a grimalkin and the Crow Witch trying to kill me, and you have interjected yourself into that situation. Last time I checked, that wasn't your fight either." Thea playfully bumped into Robin's shoulder. "Hypocrite," she teased. "Remember, there are two sides to every story. Some crazy broad keeps telling me that."

With the mood lightened, they joked and played as they made it down the dirt road to the opening in the trees, trying to forget about the past few days and the frustrations of dealing with creatures who do not listen. The ravens had finally left their sides and returned to the elves camp.

Thea's little cabin was just as she had left it so many weeks ago. Fig jumped out of the wagon and ran ahead to the porch. "Home sweet home," Robin said as she wrapped her arm around Thea's shoulder.

"If you say so."

Thea went through her books again. She knew that she had seen something about elements when she was here before. She was fanning through her books as Robin settled into the little sitting area and popped a bottle of ginger fizzy.

"It's going to take a lot of practice for you to figure out how to master the other elements," Robin stated as she kicked her feet up on the table and settled in, relaxing her tired legs and looking at home in the cabin.
Fig climbed up onto Robin's lap and stretched out for his nap.
"Ah! I found it!" Thea exclaimed. She had her nose in the book for the majority of the day while Robin napped or explored the cabin's property.

"Hey, listen to this," Thea yelled at Robin, who was fixing their dinner. "Some people are made of fire, some of water or air, or even earth. Others are made with two or three of these elements and occasionally are made with all the rare occasion elements. Think about how the hawk and the sparrow fly high in the air but flees water. The snake cannot fly and is bound to the earth as the fish can only swim." Thea stopped and looked up at Robin. "How does any of this make sense? They're comparing the animals to where they fit in the spectrum of the world…but where does fire fit in? What animal do you know can survive fire, swim in the water, walk and land and fly in the sky?" Thea questioned. Robin pulled out Thea's book of creatures and opened to one of the middle pages, and slid Thea the book to examine. "A dragon?" Thea questioned. "When have you ever seen a dragon?"

Robin just giggled in the response. "Well, you have seen nymphs, elves, fairies, mud trolls, and a Crow Witch within the last few weeks, and now you are questioning the existence of a dragon?"

Thea smirked. "Fair enough." She stated before she put her nose back in the book.

Thea read the book from cover to cover and did not find anything that told her how to tell what elements are within a witch or control them.

"You just need to focus on what you want to do and do it," Robin said to her as she took Thea's book out of her hands. "Come here," she said to Thea as she motioned for her to come to the pump sink. Robin began to pump the water into the sink and filled it about half full. She put some water onto her fingertips and flicked it at Thea. Thea flinched at the water, hitting her on the face.

"Be one with the water," Robin joked as she kept flicking beads of water at Thea's face.

"Really?" she said as she splashed the water at Robin.

"Yes. Focus." She splashed her back. Thea tried to control her emotions again and put her palms facing the water. The water started to ripple as she focused all her energy on the water. "You're doing it! Now, form it into a sphere." Robin was coaching her from the side of the tub. Thea's arm started to shake as the water began to splash around on its own. Thea let out a loud grunt, and then the water rose out of the tub and splashed over her head like a tidal wave.

She was drenched from head to toe. Robin sat there and laughed hysterically. "I'm sorry," she said as she placed a hand on Thea's shoulder. "That was hilarious!"

Thea had dried off with a towel and was sitting on the edge of the bed. "Hey, don't give up; you can at least move the water and the thunderbolts. I can only move dirt," Robin said as she rubbed her friends back in support. "Let's go outside and try to make some mud trolls." Thea nodded disappointedly as she followed Robin to the door.

Thea stood outside with her wet hair dripping, leaving wet spots on her oversized shirt. She tried to control her core once again, as she pointed her hands down at the earth like she saw Robin do in the market. The ground began to tremble under their feet.

"Work!" Thea yelled at the ground. She had tears running down her face as her body shook. Robin and Fig watched in awe as the roots started to come up through the dirt, and the ground began to form into little trolls, just as Robin had done before.

"You're doing it! You're doing it!" Robin was jumping up and down with excitement. "I told you that you were powerful enough!" The little mud trolls were marching towards Thea.

"This is amazing!" Thea yelled as she directed the trolls to march towards the field.

"I told you that you could do it," Robin said as she folded her arms across her chest and leaned back against the post of the porch.

After much practice, they were now covered in filth and were wet from head to toe. They headed back into the cabin to get cleaned up and find some dinner.

"What did you do with that necklace?" Robin said as she was digging through Thea's jewelry box.

"What necklace would that be? I doubt, I remember." Thea said with a giggle at her own joke.

"That one," Robin said as she pointed to the painting on the wall. "We need that." She said in a mumble as she continued to dig through the stuff on the bookcase.

"We need that?" Thea questioned with a raised eyebrow.

Robin stopped digging and looked up at Thea. "Huh? Oh, well, you need it. You always said that it was something important, and you shouldn't take it off." Robin was speaking slowly as if she were trying to think of how to phrase what she wanted to say.

"Good thing I have it on then," Thea said suspiciously as she pulled the necklace up from the collar of her shirt.

"Oh, good! You do have it. Let's get dinner started." Robin hurried off to the kitchen. Thea looked over to Fig and then watched her friend with a twisted look on her face.

That was weird. I wonder why this would be so important to her? She thought to herself as she felt the cool touch of the jewel against her skin.

"I wish that I could influence more elements too," Robin said as they were eating their dinner. Thea looked at her sheepishly.

"I'm sorry, I'm sure…"

Robin cut her off, "No, I can't. I've been trying ever since I found out that I have powers. It's okay, kiddo. We all have different levels of powers and can-do different things. I've always been better at brewing spells, anyway." Robin was pushing her food around on her plate with her fork. "If you want to get better training, you should go to Sorgin's place. She has been teaching witches how to control their magic for years. We can go to school to visit her." Robin was studying Thea's face as she offered up the information.

"Where is her school?" Thea asked self-consciously, wiping at her face under the scrutiny.

"The north side of the lake in Evertree Forest. Not far from here." Robin said as she pointed towards the way that Thea had initially come from when she followed Fig to her cabin.

"Well, it sounds like we now have plans for tomorrow."

The girls cleaned the house, and Robin went through Thea's stash of herbs and magical items for making potions and tonics.

"You have banshee tears? Too bad you can't remember anything; I bet that's an interesting story on how you obtained these." Robin slipped the bottle into the bag she was packing for the road. Robin was in the kitchen for most of the night as she made a potion for everything from sleeping to holding your breath longer and even making you run faster. Thea was very astonished by the amount of knowledge Robin had for potion-making. She didn't even need to look in her books for most of the potions she had made.

"Now see, I wish I could do that," Thea said. She was leaning on the table, watching Robin drop sprigs of rosemary into a couple of bottles. "Why are you making all of these potions anyway?" Thea looked confused. "Aren't we just going to a school?"

"Oh, you know, you just have so many great ingredients lying around. This can be learned. It doesn't take any special power to do. If you can read and measure out ingredients, you can make a potion," Robin said as she started to slice up an apple for some other mixture, she was making.
"I beg to differ," Thea said. "People can try to bake and never

have their cake rise in the middle. You have to have the gift to make it all work."

The girls cuddled up in the only bed in the cabin and settled in for the night. Fig seemed annoyed that he didn't fit on the bed and settled for the big blue chair, with dingy gold buttons on the edge of the fireplace. The wind howled outside the cabin as the fire was crackling across the room. Through the darkness, a crow's cry echoed outside. Both girls opened their eyes and looked at each other.

"There's got to be more than one crow in the woods," Robin whispered.

Thea rolled out of bed and peered out the window. There she was. Thalia was standing in the middle of the field, blindly stumbling around in the moonlight. She had bandages wrapped around her head where her eyes used to be. She stopped and pointed straight ahead, and started walking towards the cabin.

"Thalia," Thea whispered as she closed the blinds. Robin got up and looked out the window on the other side of the door.

"There is nothing out there," Robin said, annoyed as she staggered back to bed. Thea looked back out to the field to see nothing but the remnants of mud trolls that she had made earlier in the day.

"But I saw her," Thea said as she stared out the window a bit longer.

"Go to bed," Robin said as she rolled over next to the wall. Thea dropped another log onto the fire and then went to bed.

"I seriously saw her," Thea said as she laid her head down. Robin patted her on the head and went back to snoring.

They started at first light to see Sorgin. The witches locked the door and were on their way. Fig walked out to the center of the field and began to meow at the girls.

"What is your cat howling about?" Robin asked as she pulled a floppy hat she had found in Thea's closet over her flowing curls. Fig was still meowing as Thea walked upon him.

"What?" She said as she looked at her cat. He was standing next to a set of footprints in the mud, with two black feathers lying next to them.

"I told you I saw her," Thea said as they walked down the path, looking off to the thicket of the forest. "She's still trying to track me."

Robin had her staff out but was using it as a walking stick and did not seem very concerned about the Crow Witch. "She can't see it. I think that you have the advantage over her."

Thea stopped to adjust her knee-high boot and to pull her ponytail tighter. She saw the same little colored frogs and birds as she saw the day that she woke up. Finally, something that she could remember without her head hurting. She moved down the path, and the trio made it to the brook. They filled up all of their canteens with water before they continued.

Just after lunch, they reach the small lake where Thea had woken so many months before. "This is the place," Thea said to Robin as they walked up to the grassy patch where Thea had her first memory.

"Really?" Robin questioned as she looked around. "This isn't far from the witch school." Thea followed Robin down to the other side of the lake, where there was a wooden sign hanging from two pieces of rope tied to a branch of a tree. It was brightly painted with little daisies that said: "Chateau MelBel" with an arrow pointed down the path to the left.

"I thought you said her name was Sorgin?" Thea said as she gestured to the sign. "Mel Bel was the founder of the witches' school. They never changed the name after Sorgin took over." Robin stated. "We're almost there." Her pace quickened, and Thea had to scramble to keep up.

They continued down the path to a small lake that had a watermill turning on the side of a large stone building. "They have electricity? I thought that was only possible in the city," Thea said in awe as she looked up the six-story chateau.

"There's running water throughout the chateau, as well," Robin said with a smile. "It feels like being home." They picked up the pace as they walked onto the grounds of the chateau. The garden on either side of the walkway had blooming tulips and daisies. There were large goldfish swimming in the lake and cattails along the banks.

It looks cheery, Thea thought as they walked up the stone stairs to the door. Robin pulled on the silk rope next to the door that rang a loud bell inside the building. The clicking of someone's heels could be heard approaching the other side of the door. The door flew open, and a very handsome man answered. He had long blonde hair slicked back into a stub of a ponytail highlighting his widow's peak. His eyes were a glistening blue. He was wearing black leather pants with a flowy white shirt that hung unbuttoned to his navel.

"Uh. Hi. Is Sorgin in?" Robin was taken aback by seeing a man in the house.

"Please, come in," He said with a half-smile as he looked the women up and down. Robin removed her hat when they were in the doorway, and she fluffed her curly red hair. The man watched her with his head cocked to the side. Thea was the last to walk into the entryway. She looked around the hallway and saw beautiful paintings of landscapes and animals which were framed in gold. The rugs on the floor looked to be brand new, hand-woven, in green and blue wools. Against many of the walls were glass cases with different knick-knacks and other collectibles. One case was filled with different butterflies and another full of thimbles.

"Interesting place," Thea said as she followed the man into the parlor.

"Please wait here," The man said before he disappeared behind a curtained door.

"What's with all the different cases?" Thea whispered to Robin.

"I'm not sure; they weren't here that last time I visited," she replied as she sat down on the grand couch. Fig jumped up and sat between the two girls as they waited for Sorgin. After about twenty minutes, the man reappeared from behind the curtain, carrying a teapot and three stunning teacups, each with unique floral patterns. He poured the tea. He put a little honey and two cubes of sugar in the third cup before retreating behind the curtain again without saying a word. As the girls started to fix their own cups, they heard the clicking of someone's heels stone floor. As the steps grew louder, the curtain over the doorway opened on its own.

The woman on the other side was short with long salt and pepper hair tied up on the top of her head in a tight bun. She had a high collared button-down blouse on. The buttons were made of crystal, and the slate blue of the shirt made her hair shine. She had a well-fitted skirt that went down to her ankles, with black pointed boots sticking out from underneath. She had a brooch pinned to the pocket of the shirt. She walked with a small cane that had the sculpture of a skull for the handle. The woman paused in the doorway as if she was posing for their approval.

"Hello. How may I help you?" the woman crisply greeted them as she stoically walked over to the open seat on the couch across from the young witches.

"Sorgin? Do you remember me?" Robin asked excitedly. Sorgin pulled out a pair of glasses from her pocket and placed them on the end of her nose as she looked Robin up and down.

"Robin? Is that you, child?" Robin's face lit up as if she had been accepted to an elite club. Robin got up and crossed the coffee table to hug Sorgin. The elder witch uncomfortably hugged Robin as she lightly patted her back.

"Sorgin, this is Thea. She could use your help." Robin gestured to where Thea and Fig were sitting. Thea nervously waved her hand at Sorgin and then quickly put her hand back on her lap when she didn't see any type of acknowledgment from Sorgin.

"How do you do?" Sorgin asked as she looked Thea over. Thea smiled at her and thanked her for the tea and welcoming her into the house.

Robin told the old witch how she has been able to start conjuring with all of the elements; however, she could not control two of them. Sorgin, for the first time since the two showed up in her house, seemed to have a genuine interest in Thea being there.

"All four elements?" Sorgin questioned as she looked over the top of her glasses. "Charles?! Make up the guest rooms!" Sorgin called gently down the hall at her manservant. Thea looked around but couldn't see the man anywhere. "Show me," Sorgin said to Thea. "Show me your strongest element." Thea slowly nodded at her, feeling very intimidated by the way that Sorgin carried herself. Thea stood up, conjured a fireball in her left hand, and held it in front of her. She focused her energy on the ball and made the flames form into two people dancing in a circle as if they were at a ball. She then shook her hand, and the flame disappeared.

"You need some polishing on your timing, but very well done. It will take some time to train you," Sorgin said. She smiled for the first time.

Robin was up and moving around the room, looking out the windows and peaking down the halls. "Where is everyone?" Robin questioned. "There's usually creatures and witches all over the grounds."

Sorgin shook her head no. "This hasn't been a school in fifteen years. I'm just a retired lady in a big house. Come, I'll show you around."

The girls uneasily looked at Sorgin's many collection cases, and her paintings hung on the walls as Sorgin recounted, where she got each item and explained how priceless each one was. This continued through dinner. They ate at a proper dining room table and had quail with roasted potatoes.

"Thank you, Charles," Robin said as he placed a bowl of pudding in front of her for dessert. Sorgin was still talking about her collections and rambling on how she got her silverware from a gnome, who got caught in a trap out in the forest; Sorgin had released him.

When dinner ended, Sorgin led them to the back of the house. "This is where we will practice," Sorgin said to Thea. "We will start tomorrow at nine precisely." Thea looked about the backyard, which was on the shore of the lake. There were ducks in the bay and a large, red barn on the bank. "I don't suppose you would be alright with the cat staying out there in the barn?" Sorgin asked as she sent a dirty look to Fig.

"I prefer that he stays with me," Thea responded quickly.

"I supposed that would be fine; he is housebroken, isn't he?" she said condescendingly towards the cat. Fig growled in the direction of Sorgin.

"He's a great cat; he'll be well behaved," Robin chimed in, as she shot Fig a look to behave himself.

Thea enjoyed watching Robin as she followed Sorgin around. She seemed star-struck as she attempted to get Sorgin's attention. Yet something was off.

Sorgin had retired early and left the girls alone in the parlor.

"This is strange, Robin. I feel horribly uncomfortable here." Thea said as she carried Fig over to the couch. "This woman seems more concerned about how to impress you with what she has, instead of remembering who you are."

"She doesn't seem the same," Robin stated, with a perplexed look on her face. "She uses to be so full of life and excited to teach. I wonder what happened to her."

They heard Charles clear his throat from the doorway. "Follow me to your rooms, please." He said as he led the girls out of the parlor. They walked up the stairs to the third floor of the building and found gorgeous suites with conjoining doors between the rooms. Thea's had an actual lamp and its own bathroom attached to it. The bed had a canopy with curtains that made the bed look like a fancy tent. Fig hopped down out of her arms, ran over to the bench next to the window, and looked out.

"Good evening, Miss," Charles said as he shut the door. She heard a click of the door behind him. Thea went over and opened the door between their rooms.

"Did he just lock us in here? Like we can't leave our rooms?" Robin crept over to the door and jiggled the handle. It was, in fact, locked.

"What the hell is going on?" Thea questioned.

"I'm not sure," Robin said with the sound of panic in her voice.
The girls paced the rooms and started to push on every window and even the walls. The windows were painted shut, and the walls were solid stone.

There didn't seem to be any way out.

"I could set the door on fire?" Thea stated as she started to create a fireball. Robin grabbed Thea's arm and shook her flameout.

"You need Sorgin's help to remember your abilities. I don't think she'll be willing to help you if you set her house on fire," Robin said rationally, trying to calm Thea down.

"She locked us up in these rooms like we're animals! Why would she do this?" Thea was starting to get louder while Robin got quieter. "I don't like being forced to stay anywhere!" Robin began to hush Thea by putting her finger to her lips.

"Listen. Did you hear that?" Robin whispered. "There's a scraping from behind that wall." Robin's voice was barely audible, but Fig clearly heard the noise, too; Thea couldn't hear anything. Fig had his ears perked up and was over at the wall, sniffing at the floorboard. The little cat followed the noise across the floor to the corner of the wall as it disappeared.

"I really don't feel good about any of this." Thea started to rub her temple. Robin went over to her bag and gave her some of the arrowroot dust tonics. "Thanks," Thea said before she took a swig out of the bottle.

"Well, we're at least stuck here for the night. We might as well settle in." Robin said with a shrug. Thea was concerned by Robin's lack of concern.

"We're staying in the same room," Thea answered back as she picked up Fig and walked into Robin's room. The girls crawled into the soft fluff of the bed with Fig standing guard above their heads. Thea had the unsettling feeling that they were being watched. She ended up tossing and turning throughout the night without much actual sleep.

As she lay there, Thea finally heard the scraping that the others had heard before. She got out of bed and walked over to the wall. The floor was icy on her bare feet as she walked on her tiptoes across the room. She pressed her ear up to the wall below the portrait of some noble prince. The noise had stopped again, but Fig was now up and had followed Thea over to where she stood. He jumped up onto the bookcase next to her and meowed as he stared up at the painting.

"Shhhhh..." she hushed the cat as she was trying to listen. He meowed again and then stretched up the wall, trying to climb up to what caught his attention. Thea followed where the gaze of the cat was fixated. She looked up just in time to see the portrait's eyes make eye contact with her, and then the eyes flashed away, disappearing behind the wall. Thea's blood-curdling scream echoed through the massive chateau.

Chapter Fifteen

Robin jumped up from a dead sleep and ran over to Thea. "What?! Why are you screaming?" Thea pointed up to the painting.

"The eyes moved! Someone is watching us from the wall!" Thea snapped at Robin. The eyes of the painting were back to being the originals of the image.

"You were dreaming. There is nothing wrong with that painting," Robin said with a stretch and yawn.

Thea's expression hardens as she looked back at Robin. "Give me a boost." Thea started to climb up the wall. Robin rolled her eyes, bent down with cupped hands, and gave her a boost. Thea reached up to the eyes of the painting and poked them. The fillers holding the eyes in place fell backward into the wall leaving two black gaping holes.

"See?! Someone is watching us!" Thea hissed in a hushed whisper.

"Seriously?" Robin questioned with fear in her voice. Thea grabbed Robin's hand and swooped Fig up in her arm; they hustled over to Thea's canopy bed and shut the curtains around them.

"We leave in the morning," Thea said as she peered out through the curtain. "This is really flipping creepy," Thea whispered.

They took turns sleeping through the night and were up, dressed, and ready to go when the sun came up the next morning. They heard footsteps approach the doors at eight o'clock, each lock clicked, and then footsteps retreating down the hallway. Thea opened the door a crack and peered out into the hall. It was empty in both directions.

"Let's go!" she signaled back to Robin and Fig. They descended the stairs and were headed to the door.

Thea had her hands on the doorknob when she heard Sorgin's voice, "Leaving so soon?" Thea whipped around to face the old witch with her hand out on her side and ready to attack. "Oh, I don't recommend that. I'm much stronger than you are," she said, as she gestured to Thea's hand.

"We don't appreciate being locked in a room and spied on," Thea had hatred in her voice. Robin was moving closer to the door.

"I have two strangers show up to my home, and you expect me to trust you to run free while I sleep?" Sorgin's voice was calm as she leaned on her skull handled cane.

"I'll manage learning magic on my own, thank you," stated Thea as she opened the front door. Robin gave Sorgin a worried glance as she started to follow Thea outside.

The two young witches and the little orange cat made their way onto the lawn. As they neared the walking path to head back to Thea's cabin, the sky turned grey, and the air had an icy chill. Thea blew out her breath to be seen in a billow of smoke. A gust of wind blew hard enough to blow the girls over. There was a crack of thunder that echoed in their ears, followed by the cry of a crow. Thea's head started to throb as they looked to where the noise came from. Down on the edge of the water was Thalia. She had a thunderbolt in her hand and was pointing directly at Thea, as though she could see where she was.

"Thea!" Thalia yelled in a commanding voice. "You have tried to destroy my coven! You have taken my eyes! You have destroyed my cousin and made her a monster! Your wickedness must be stopped, and you will be destroyed!" Thalia was hysterically screaming at Thea; the thunderbolt in her hand grew brighter with her anger.

"Thalia," Thea held her hands up in front of her in protest. "I did none of those things. The ravens took your eyes, not me. I do not know about doing anything to your coven or your cousin. You have to believe me. If I did you or anyone harm, I am so completely sorry." Tears were forming in the corners of Thea's eyes as she pleaded with the Crow Witch. "I have one of your eyes right here," she said as she pulled the bottle out of her bag.

"I won't fall for your tricks again, Thea!" Thalia screamed at the top of her lungs. "I promised my coven I would bring you back to save Lilly, and I plan on doing just that!"

Robin stood in front of her friend and brought her hands from her sides to in front of her. The ground shook, and hundreds of small dirt trolls marched out of the earth and started to stack one on top of the other. They formed one large troll that was as large as the chateau. It ripped out a tree from the ground and held it in front of the girls as a sword. Thea's eyes grew red with emotion as she brought a fireball to her hand.

"Thalia, we are not going to figh…" Thea couldn't get her words out before Thalia blindly launched a thunderbolt in their direction. It was a direct hit through the heart of the mud troll, sending mud and the tree flying through the air. They were covered from head to toe with the filth that passed through the air. Thea launched her fireball over Robin's shoulder, and it landed in front of Thalia's feet, setting the grass around her ablaze.

"Thalia, I'm begging you! Please, stop!" Thalia laughed at the sky as she had conjured another thunderbolt and shot it at the girls again. This one hit Robin on her foot, sending electric shocks throughout her body. Robin's fiery hair was standing out, and her body shook uncontrollably as she was being electrocuted.

"No!" Thea screamed as she dove on her friend, rolling her on the ground.

Thalia's laughter grew louder as another figure came out of the forest, walking over next to her. She had fair skin and short blonde hair that was so light it looked to be white. She placed her hand on Thalia's shoulder and raised her other hand high above her head. The lake's water started to rise over the tops of the trees, creating a wall between the forest and the chateau.

"Robin, wake up!" Thea said as she shook her friend. She felt the now-familiar surge of energy running through her and into Robin's shoulders. Robin's head lifted off the ground, and her eyes opened as she gasped for air. Thea let go of her friend and stood up to face Thalia and the other witch. She felt weak and woozy from healing Robin. Thea brought her arm out from her side and stared ahead. Hatred filled her stomach as she focused all emotions on this one conjuring. She had to save her friend. Thea started to lift her arm to aim at Thalia, but she lost her balance and fell over. Her head was pounding. She grabbed her head as she tried to stand again. She reached out and found her staff to use as a crutch and lift herself up.

She looked up to see the blonde hair of Charles running towards the Crow Witch from around the backside of the water wall, with a sword raised above his head. He got close enough to the witches that he swung his sword, nicking the pale witch across her cheek. As he raised his sword again, Thalia reached out one arm and grabbed Charles by his neck. She was strong enough to lift him off his feet. Thalia reached up to Charles' face with her free hand and snatched out his icy blue eye. He screamed in pain and dropped his sword as he fell to the ground, clutching his face. Thalia removed the wrappings from her face and inserted Charles' eyeball into her empty socket. She blinked twice and looked directly at Thea with a devilish smile spreading across her lips.

The witches laughed as they bent down to Charles' face. Thalia swiftly kicked Charles in the ribs with the tip of her pointed boot. He groaned in pain as she pulled back for another shot. A blue streak of light flashed between him and the witches just as Thea had propelled an immense fireball straight at Thalia.

The fireball hit her in the arm and knocked her over into the other witch. Robin was back to her feet and had Thalia and her friend surrounded with mud trolls.

"Not today!" yelled the blonde witch as she hurled her water wall towards the group.

Another wisp of blue light came between the witches and Thalia – it grew to a large bubble that surrounded Thea, Robin, and the chateau. Thea looked over her shoulder towards the chateau. Sorgin was standing there with both hands raised above her head, her cane in her left hand pointed towards Thalia. The skull was glowing a dark purple as the blue light of the bubble engulfed the sky. Her face was stern and fixated ahead. The water wall that had started to crash towards the chateau hit the force field and fell back onto the blonde witch and Thalia. The mud trolls had begun to jump onto the two witches, who were gasping for air. As the water hit the trolls, they turned back to mud, partially covering the witches. The blonde-haired witch screamed in a high enough pitch it burst out the windows in the chateau, sending shards of glass flying through the air. She raised her arm, and she and Thalia were immersed in a screen of red smoke. When the smoke had cleared, they were gone.

Sorgin lowered her cane, and the blue light retreated into the skull. She walked over to Charles and helped him up. Thea and

Robin were in shock and panting as they lifted themselves with their staff.

"Heal him," Sorgin demanded as she grabs Thea's hand. Thea nodded as she placed her hand on his face. The blood that was streaked down his cheek became moist and rolled up his face to the socket. The skin around his eye grew over the wound. Thea let out a moan and fell back, panting.

"Are you ready to learn now?" Sorgin questioned as she smoothed down her hair and adjusted her skirt. Thea looked over to Robin and raised her eyebrows before her eyes rolled back into her head, and she gracefully fainted down to the grass. Robin crawled over to her friend and wiped the mud away from Thea's mouth as she cradled her head.

"You two are weak," Sorgin said as she turned and started to walk back towards the chateau with Charles in tow. "Still think you can handle this on your own?"

The girls sat out on the chateau's lawn for a few hours as Thea slowly woke up. The mud and filth had now hardened in the sun and was caked onto them. Fig had emerged from wherever he had disappeared to during their latest encounter with Thalia. Thea opened her eyes and started to blink in the sun. She raised her hand to block the light.

"Only out a few hours this time," Robin said to Thea as she stroked her hair. Fig was sitting on her chest, looking down on her face.

"Thanks for the help, cat," Thea said sarcastically as she patted the cat on the head. "What the hell just happened?" she asked.

"Well, Thalia is pissed….at you." Robin said cynically as she pointed down at her friend. "And we suck at magic, and Sorgin had to save our butts…and"

Thea cut her off. "It was rhetorical, Robin."

Thea sat up and took a look around the yard. There was a giant oak tree uprooted, lying in the middle of the lawn. There were muddy puddles all over what used to be a well-maintained yard.

"I wanted to wait until you woke up to see what you wanted to do. Sorgin has mockingly invited us to stay by telling us how weak we are," Robin said as she held out her left hand. "On the other hand, I pretty much died, and then you had to save me, which means that you weren't strong enough to take care of yourself. And, multiple witches are trying to kill you." She started to lift both her hands up and down like they were the scales of justice.

"So, we either stay locked up in the old witch's house and be protected, or we venture out by ourselves and continue to be stalked by the Crow Witch and her coven." Thea pushed the cat off of her and pulled herself up with her staff. "Well, I guess we are going to swallow our pride and ask for help. Come on." She offered Robin a hand. "Let's go eat our humble pie." They limped back to the house and lightly knocked on the front door. After a few minutes of waiting, Charles answered the door sporting a new leather eye patch.

"Charles! Oh, Charles, I am…oh, I am so sorry you got hurt. Thank you for protecting us." Robin stammered. Thea looked at him with tears in her eyes and touched his shoulder. He solemnly nodded at the girls as he gestured for them to come in.

The girls stood in the hallway and heard Sorgin's heels clicking on the stone floor as she came around the corner. "I see you have decided to come in from the yard," Sorgin said with a smirk on her face. She stood with both hands resting on her cane.

Thea swallowed hard. "Sorgin, thank you for your assistance out there," she started. "I have no idea why she is hunting me; I seriously do not remember anything that has happened up to a few months ago. Can we try training with you….please?" Thea could not meet the glare of Sorgin as she spoke.

"The two of you are weak. I don't know if you have what it takes to become powerful enough to handle those two witches, let alone a coven and a grimalkin," Sorgin replied. "You cost Charles his eye and wrecked my yard. That grimalkin tore up my barn and chased off my horses last night, too."

The girls lowered their chins in surprise as they looked at each other. "The Grimalkin was here last night?" Thea questioned.

"Look at the side of the barn," Sorgin instructed as she led them to a window. The barn outside had big swipes taken out of the sidewall. Thea had an uneasy feeling in her stomach. She looked at all the destruction caused by the two of them being at the chateau.

"Sorgin, I don't know what to say," Thea stated as she looked into the old witch's face.

"Go up to your rooms, get cleaned up, and rest. We will start tomorrow." Sorgin said as she walked past them and over to one of the many cases against the wall. She took out of her cleavage a small glass bottle that had a blue light trapped inside of it, placing it in the case, and shut the door. "Charles, please show them to their rooms."

Charles had fresh towels in his hands and was waiting at the foot of the stairs for the girls. They slowly climbed to the same rooms they were in before. Charles shut the door behind them as they entered, and again, there was a click of the lock from the outside. New pajamas were laid out on both beds for them. "I feel like I'm in one of her cases," Robin said sarcastically as she walked into her bathroom and shut the door.

Thea drew a bath and filled it with bubbles. Fig sat on the edge of the tub, playing with them as they floated over the side of the tub. Thea rested and soaked until the hot water had turned cold, and the bubbles had been replaced with a muddy ring. She washed her hair and rolled it up in a towel before scrubbing her dirt ring out of the tub, then putting on the pink striped pajamas. She looked into the mirror and examined the bruises she had received in battle. She looked tired and defeated. Thea walked out to find a tray with sandwiches, fruit, and water left on the table in her room.

She poked her head into Robin's room and saw her looking out the window in her matching pajamas. "Charles left us lunch," Thea said as she motioned with her head to the table in her room.

"Look," Robin was pointing down to the grounds. Thea hurried over to the window to see a man in a jumpsuit leading a unicorn and a bear cub into the barn.

Once they were in the barn, the little man slid the latch into place and locked the door.

"Seems to be the theme around here," Thea whispered as she looked around the room. Robin had hung her towels over the portraits on the walls. "Good idea." Thea chuckled as she nudged Robin to come to eat.

Thea followed suit with her towels and hung them over the paintings in her room as well. Sitting in silence for the majority of their meal, watching out the window as the man in the jumpsuit worked. He collected a couple of horses and what Robin thought to be a griffin, adding them to the barn. The two girls decided it was time for them to get some sleep and rest their bodies before they had to train the next day.

When Thea woke up, she was sore, and her throat was dry; she must have been snoring all night. Fig was wrapped around the top of her head, purring softly. She reached up and scratched his ears before she sat up. She pulled back the curtain of the canopy bed to see fresh clothes hanging on the door of the closet and breakfast sitting on her table. A chill ran down her back at the thought of someone in her room while she slept.

She got up and walked over to the door to Robin's room, who was getting dressed in long flowy black pants and a smock-like shirt. There was slide on canvas shoes there as well. Thea sleepily waved at Robin as she covered her mouth with her other hand to yawn.

"Morning," Robin said. "Do I smell bacon?"

Thea nodded. "Charles brought a whole spread over," She went back in her room and changed into her outfit matching Robin. "How did they know my shoe size?" Thea asked out loud.

"I was wondering the same thing," Robin replied, chewing on a piece of crispy bacon. "Is the door unlocked?"

"I don't know," Thea walked over and turned the knob expecting to feel resistance, and to her surprise, the door opened. They ate their breakfast of pancakes, eggs, pudding, and bacon before adventuring out of the room and heading down the stairs. Charles waited at the bottom of the stairs. He gave them a nod of his head before walking to the back of the house.

"Curious man, isn't he?" Robin said as she watched him walk through a door, then heard the click of the lock behind him.

Robin and Thea continued to the sitting room, where they saw Sorgin waiting for them. "It's about time that you got up! We have work to do." The old witch was dressed in an outrageous dress of plaid and flowers. Her hair was in a long braid over one of her shoulders, and she was wearing a pair of specks that were neon orange. "Outside, though. I don't want you two messing up my house like you did the yard."

Thea inwardly sighed*; if the day was going to start with a scolding, what would happen during the training?*

Sorgin led them to the muddy front yard and had them start off facing each other. "Now, you two have to get some confidence that you have abilities. You are stronger than you think you are, but you are not properly executing the spells because of it. You are hesitating." The girls looked at Sorgin like she was crazy

"The feeling that you get in the pit of your stomach when you are stressed, sad, pissed off… that is your power that you don't know how to use." Sorgin started pacing back and forth as she spoke to the girls. Fig sat on the ground between them and watched the old witch. "Most people just brush it off as nerves. Witches can use that as power. Having control over your emotions is the art of conjuring." She stopped right in front of Robin. "You have the unique talent with tonics and potions, yet you waste your time with little things like arrowroot dust? You should be making cures for people's ailments, not just quick pain relievers." Sorgin then turned and looked at Thea. "But you! You have power like I have never seen. Thea, you might have the power of the fifth element." The girls gave her a curious look.

"I'm sorry, what would that be?" Robin wondered. "There are water, fire, earth, and wind. I'm pretty sure that there aren't any more to be had."

Sorgin pushed one arm out from her cane and sent Robin flying backward, landing on her butt. "The Ether," Sorgin stated as she calmly put her hand back onto the skull. "Everything and anything that is between those elements can be used as a spell too. She has it." Sorgin was pointing a perfectly manicured finger at Thea.

"How would you know that?" Thea asked nervously as she helped Robin to her feet.

"I can sense it in you. Now we need to get you to sense it too." They spent the better part of the day conjuring baby dirt trolls, fireballs, thunderbolts, and water spheres. It was not going well. The girls were failing miserably, and Sorgin was losing patience.

"I think you need some better motivation." Sorgin eventually said as she looked at them over the brim of her glasses. She circled the girls and lifted her cane. Robin went flying up into a blue bubble, high above Thea's head. "You better focus on that thunderbolt before Robin loses all her air," Sorgin said without a trace of emotion. Robin was banging on the bubble as if she was enclosed in glass. Thea could tell she was screaming but couldn't hear a sound.

"What are you doing to her?!" Thea was panicked.

"That is what I call motivation, Thea. Your friend is running out of time; you'd better hurry up." Again, there was a concerning lack of emotion from the old witch.

Thea raised her arm in the air and brought forth a fireball. Sorgin waved her hand at Thea and knocked her over with an unseen force. "I SAID…. THUNDERBOLT! Listen to me, Child or your friend dies!"

Thea jumped up, raised her hand to the sky, and started to tremble with the force of the wind. Robin was holding her chest and gasping for air; her face was visibly turning blue. The sky turned grey as a small thunderbolt formed in Thea's hand. She hurled it into the air at the blue bubble, shattering it into tiny shards as Robin fell from the sky. Sorgin tilted her head back and cackled. "See Child? You just needed motivation."

This torturous training continued for weeks. They would wake in the morning, put on clothes that were laid out for them, practice all day, then return to their confines with a lock of the door. It got to the point where the girls stopped checking the door in the middle of the night to see if they could get out. They accepted that this was where they were right now.

Their practice was going so well that Robin could now conjure both water and earth with great ease; her eyes rarely turned colors anymore when she was casting a spell. She even worked on her potions with Sorgin. She was now able to turn Fig into a frog with one of her elixirs.

Thea was on her way to mastering all five elements. She could fling objects just by moving her hand and conjuring up mud trolls and making trees start walking; she could even control the water. Thea's problem was that it took a lot out of her body; her stamina was not where it needed to handle conjuring for long periods. Sorgin had informed her that was a common problem amongst witches. Thea and Robin also continued to work with their staff to study self-defense because they still didn't feel confident in their powers.

After a day of intense training, the girls retired to their rooms as usual. Charles had laid out a fresh set of pajamas and their dinner for them. He was still in the room when the girls walked in. "Oh, thank you, Charles." Robin chimed at him. He did his standard head nod before leaving the room. Thea noticed a dark bracelet on his wrist that looked like it was cutting into his skin.

"Do you need help loosening that?" Thea reached for his wrist, but she got a painful shock and pulled her arm back when she touched it. Charles just sadly nodded his head and then left the room. The lock clicked behind him. "Did you see that?" Thea was shaking her hand. She had a red burn on her fingers. Robin held Thea's hand and applied a tingly potion to her burn, and it quickly healed.

"That was strange. Almost as strange as Charles is," Robin mumbled dismissively.

The girls had their dinner, then went to sleep. It was around three in the morning when Thea awoke to the lock on the door clicking. She laid there for a moment behind the curtains of the bed, listening for footsteps that never came. Thea poked her head out of the curtain; only a dim light came in from under the door.

"Did you hear that?" Robin whispered to Thea. She had crept into Thea's room and was standing next to her bed. Thea jumped and almost fell out of bed.

"Don't do that!" Thea hissed as she smacked Robin in the arm.
"Sorry… I think the door is unlocked!" she whispered back to her.

They put their shoes on and crept to the door. Thea held her breath as she slowly turned the handle. The door opened. The girls looked at each other for a moment before Thea opened the door for the rest of the way. They stuck their heads out the door looking in the opposite directions – the coast was clear. They slowly creeped out, not knowing what to do.

"Who let us out?" Thea questioned. Robin shrugged and held

her finger to her lips as she motioned for Thea to follow her. They started an adventure to the staircase and went up a floor, where they had never been permitted.

There were lights on. They walked past a few locked doors and then found a small end table that had a key on it.

"But which door?" Robin whispered. One by one, the girls started to try the doors, but none of them opened. They descended past their level to the second floor. They went up against each hall, testing the doors until the key slid in and clicked the lock mechanism on a plain wooden door at the end of the hallway. The girls had devilish smiles as they slowly turned the knob. They stepped into the room and turned on the light. Both girls gasped as the light shown what was in the room.

There were hundreds of jars with small creatures trapped inside. They were alive. They immediately started to pound on their containers when they saw the girls. Each jar had air holes poked in the top, but the lids had some sort of enchantment on them that shocked the girls when they tried to open them. The creatures were pounding, scratching, and running into the glass – trying to get out.

"Who did this to you?" The girls were asking the fairies, wisps, and trolls locked in that room, but they were too distracted to answer.

"Sorgin!" one of the fairies finally squeaked out.

"Sorgin?" Thea questioned in a whisper to Robin. The girls attempted opening all of the jars without any success. "I'm sorry, I can't get you out," Thea whispered over the top of the jars. The girls continued for a while and then realized that it was getting to be daylight, and they had to get back to their rooms before it was noticed that they were missing. "We'll come back," Thea promised as they headed out the door, locking it behind them. She tied the key to the inside drawstring of her pants.

They cautiously went back up the stairs to the third floor and their rooms. As they rounded a corner and started down the hall, they heard footsteps behind them. They picked up their pace and had started a soft jog when they heard: "Where are you supposed to be right now?"

Chapter Sixteen

The girls turned around to face Sorgin. She was standing in the dim hallway wearing a robe, and as always, carried her skull-headed walking cane. Thea could feel her face turning flush. "We thought we heard the Grimalkin outside." Robin said, thinking quickly, "We wanted to make sure that it didn't destroy your property, Sorgin. But we didn't see anything from our windows, so we wanted to look out the other side of the house. I apologize for not being in our rooms; we will head back there right now." She feigned a casual walk backward, away from Sorgin, and towards the bedroom door.

Sorgin was not buying it. She looked at them with one eyebrow raised over the rim of her glasses. She raised her hand and held Robin in the air by her throat without touching her. "How did you get out of your room?" She questioned.

"We picked the lock," Thea chimed in since Robin could not speak. "We didn't know how else to get ahold of you."

Sorgin studied her face for a moment before dropping Robin in a gasping heap on the floor. "NEVER do that again," Sorgin threatened as she shoved past the girls to wait by their bedroom door.

"You alright?" Thea rushed to help Robin. She was rubbing her throat and gently nodded.

They entered their rooms, with Sorgin locking the doors behind them. There was no breakfast served that morning and no practice that day.

Dinner came later than usual and was very minimal. Charles dropped the plates on the table in a rush, then quickly retreated out of the room. Thea tried to stop him and asked in a hushed, urgent tone, "Charles? Are you trapped here, or does she pay you to work?" He briefly looked up, making eye contact with

Thea. She could see the sadness there. His eyes nervously flitted up to the portrait on the wall, then to the open door, then scurried out to the hallway without answering or looking back. The click of the lock followed.

"Did you see that, Robin? He is being forced to work here against his will. He's a slave!"

"How do you suppose we are going to get out of here?" Robin questioned, bringing to light their similar predicament.

"And, how are we going to get everyone else out of here?" Thea referenced the other captives.

With no answer forthcoming, the girls sat watching the back yard as they ate their dinner, feeling more trapped than ever. Fig scratched at the door, wanting to go out. He was used to being in the yard during their practices. "Sorry, baby boy, we're stuck in here." Thea laid down a towel for Fig in the bathroom and went back to sitting at the table, reading her books, looking for answers. Robin was pacing the room and looking out the window. She was deep in thought, trying to figure out an escape.

"Gum," Thea said, as the thought came to her.

"Huh?" Robin questioned back, clearly not following.

"If we put gum in the latch of the door the next time it's unlocked, it won't lock when we are put to bed. That way, Charles won't have to unlock the door for us, and we won't risk getting him in any trouble."

Robin smiled. "Couldn't you just throw a fireball through it?"

Thea laughed at Robin. "I tried already. I think she has an enchantment on the doors."

"What about all the other doors? We can't leave everyone else here," Thea looked up from her book in surprise at Robin.

"What happened to not getting involved in things that aren't our battles? Not our fight?"

Robin shrugged her shoulders. "Maybe you're just wearing off on me."
The next morning came. The door was unlocked, their clothes were laid out, and breakfast was on the table like normal. "We must have been forgiven," Robin said with a smirk.

The girls didn't have any gum in their bags, but Robin did have some more arrowroot. She made it into a paste and stuffed it into the latch before they went down for their day. The girls did their eight hours of training out in the yard and even did some yard work. Sorgin was keeping an incredibly close eye on them and did not leave their sides.

When they were done, they went back to their rooms to bathe and have their dinners.

"Did it work?" Thea whispered to Robin. She nodded back slowly, testing the handle.

They waited until midnight and then felt ready to sneak out of the chateau. "Let's go," Thea announced as she had all the bags packed and ready.

"What about everyone else?" Robin asked. Thea stopped with her hand on the door handle.

"We can't get them out, I don't know how to get them out of their jars….and who knows how many other things she has locked up around here. We need to worry about ourselves." Thea was very annoyed as Robin hadn't cared to be bothered with anyone else before this. They had no plan, and Thea was terrified of being trapped here any longer.

"Well, you and the cat can leave, but I'm going to let them out!" With that statement, Robin was out of the room and headed down the hall.

"Take the key," Thea hush-yelled lobbed the key at her. Robin caught it and then disappeared down the stairs.
Thea made it to the front door and had her hand on the handle when she stopped. Fig looked up to her and meowed. "I know. I can't leave her," she said to the cat as she turned and walked back upstairs. Thea found Robin in the room with all the captured creatures, but Robin wasn't trying to free them; she was trying to open the door to the adjoining room. "What are you doing now?"

Robin nearly jumped out of her skin. "Holy buckets! Don't do that!" Robin turned back to the door, continuing work on getting it open.

"What are you doing now?" Thea asked as she went to try to break open the jars.

"There's more in here….I can hear them," Robin replied.

The lights flickered on. A gasp from both the girls and the creatures, as they all turned, seeing Sorgin standing at the door, her hands resting on her cane.

"NOW, what do you two think you are doing? Found another grimalkin to chase?" Sorgin did not look amused as she looked over the top of her glasses at the two young witches. Thea had backed up to where Robin was standing and was raising her hand from her hip. She started to create a massive fireball in her left hand.

"Why do you have all of these creatures trapped in here, Sorgin?" Thea asked with a furrowed brow. "They don't want to be here anymore, Sorgin, and frankly, neither do I! Let them out!"

Sorgin tilted her head back and laughed at Thea. "Let them out? Let them out?" Sorgin question as she was pointing at the bottles and jars on the shelves. Thea raised her hand, about to launch her fire directly at the laughing witch when she was tackled, falling on top of her own fireball. Thea's shirt caught fire. As Robin snuffed it out and then leaned over the top of Thea and whispered, "I'm sorry," before dropping a few drops from a bottle onto Thea's arms. She lost the feeling in her arms. The paralysis spread through her entire body. Fig jumped onto Robin's back and attacked her with his claws and teeth; he ripped Robin's dress and drew blood before she flung him against the wall with a thud.

"I lived up to my end of the bargain. Let my sister go, Sorgin."

Thea moved her eyes to look at the two witches as they were talking. Thea could see part of the skin on Robin's back where Fig had ripped her dress; the holes revealed a tattoo of a dragon with a flame coming out of its mouth, just as the drawing in Thea's spellbook had shown.

"You promised me a supreme! We've been working with her for weeks, and that hasn't been enough! Her powers are barely developing. She's no supreme," Sorgin said as she nodded towards Thea, who was lying uselessly on the floor. "I think that you are a confused little witch. This is not a fair trade for your sister, not even a fair trade for you."

Thea couldn't believe what she was hearing. Did Robin lead her here on purpose? As a trade? Thea could feel the anger boiling inside of her. "You said if I brought you, Thea, you would let Robin go!" Robin yelled. Thea was so frustrated by her paralyzed state, but was she losing her senses as well? Did she just say her sister's name is Robin? Thea was able to groan, but the two witches ignored her and continued to argue.

"I will add her to my collection, but she is not worth a trade. You owe me a powerful witch. Go catch me that Crow Witch, then perhaps I will let your sister go," Sorgin said as she shooed the girl dismissively away with her hand. The witch that Thea knew as Robin was furious; her face turned the same shade of red as her hair.

"That's what you did the last two times! Let her go!" She lifted her hands, and the bottles on the shelves began to wobble as she was conjuring a thunderbolt. "I will bring your whole house down if I have to!" Sorgin whipped her hand up and sent Robin flying into the wall and held her there. "Little Witch. Little Agatha. You are not strong enough to stand up to me! You cannot defeat me!" Sorgin cackled.

Thea, meanwhile, started to regain feeling in her feet. *Could the potion be wearing off already?* She began to wiggle her toes to get the blood flowing. Soon she was able to move her pinky finger.

"We had a blood oath, Sorgin! BLOOD!" Agatha let out a scream.

Thea took a chance and clumsily got to her feet. She was able to launch a fireball straight at Sorgin's head. Sorgin dropped Agatha in an attempt to block the blast. Agatha crashed down onto a bookshelf; some of the bottles containing the fairies crashed on the floor; however, they did not shatter.

The flame took over the entire body of the old witch, but she did not seem to be in pain. She bent over like she was sobbing, and then the sobbing turned to mystical laughter. When Sorgin opened her eyes, they were no longer icy blue but were as yellow as a dandelion with slits for pupils. Purple smoke started to billow out of her nose, and she began to fill the room with her size. She sprouted wings, and her withered skin turned to scales in hues of blue and green. She threw her cane off to the side, bending forward as she grew, now standing on all fours. Her nose changed into a rounded snout, and she had a long lizard-like tongue, which split on the tip. Sorgin's laugh turned to a resounding echo that came from her belly. Her cane started to move on its own from where it landed. It slithered like a snake, making its way to Sorgin's now ample arm; the cane fused to her skin. All that could be seen as the glowing skull embedded into her scales. She took a breath, sucking in all of the fire which had been engulfing her, into her mouth, then blew it out in full force at Thea and Agatha. A window on the wall shattered as the girls dove out of the way. A demonic growl came from the throat of the dragon before she grabbed the two girls in her claws, pushing them through the broken glass, throwing the girls onto the lawn below. Fig rushed to the gaping hole left in the wall and watched in terror as the dragon swooped out after them. Sorgin hovered over the girls before gracefully glided to the yard.

The girls had fallen hard but were able to get up and hobbled off to the forest for coverage. "What do we do?" Agatha asked Thea.

"DO?! WE?! You just tried to give me to a dragon as payment! THERE IS NO TEAM HERE!" Thea hissed as she started to conjure some mud trolls to assist with the attack.

"Thea, listen, Robin is your friend and my sister! Sorgin is a collector and has my sister locked somewhere in the chateau! I'm sorry I tricked you, but I didn't know what else to do to get her out of there." Agatha started to sob as she hid behind a bush.

Thea rolled her eyes and pushed her arms out at her sides. "That's a great sign of integrity; trick the girl who lost her memory. Just stay the hell away from me!" Thea snapped at the crying girl.

The ground began to rumble, harder than it ever had when Thea was using magic. Sorgin had launched a stream of fire over the tops of the trees, igniting the forest in a glorious blaze. Thea stood her ground and conjured up a single mud troll that was as large as Sorgin in her dragon form. He stoically walked towards Sorgin and swung at her with his mighty fist.

"Hey! You stay here and make your mud trolls to take her out at the legs. Do you think you can handle that?" Thea yelled over her shoulder at Agatha. She didn't wait for answers as she made her way behind the dragon, past the chateau, and to the other side of the waterfront. Thea already knew that her fireballs did not hurt the mighty dragon, but perhaps some water would. She raised a wall of water and sent it flying down upon the dragon.

Sorgin, the dragon, roared as her stream of fire was extinguished. The giant mud troll continued to march towards her, pounding her long neck regardless of how many times he was knocked down. Agatha had sent an army of mini mud trolls attacking Sorgin's feet and surrounding her legs so that she couldn't move. She let out another stream of fire, burning the trees in the yard. Hit after hit, Sorgin did not show any signs of weakening. She continued to laugh a demonic laugh between her attacks on the girls.

Thea, however, was starting to feel the fatigue of the battle and wasn't sure how much more she could take. She began to look for an escape route but was stuck by a firewall that circled behind her. Sorgin swung her great neck, knocking the giant mud troll over for the final time – splattering him into large clumps of mud that were shooting as projectiles throughout the yard.

Sorgin took an intense sniff into the air, then swung her head towards where Thea was hiding.

"Come out, come out where ever you are," Sorgin hissed as she lowered her head. The dragon shook her legs and broke the packs of mud around her feet. Thea started to panic; she had nowhere to run. She brought forth a thunderbolt that illuminated the night's sky with such power that Sorgin's face cringed with pain as the electricity connected with her head, traveling down her scaly body to the wet grass. Thea could see Agatha trying to conjure the water from the other side of the yard. She was failing miserably; all she was doing was creating waves in the lake. Thea felt her fight against the dragon was hopeless.

Sorgin lunged towards the forest, biting at the air as she tried to attack Thea. Luckily, the dragon barely missed her by just a few feet, though Thea still got swiped by the tail when the dragon spun around. Lying face down on the trampled earth, Thea suddenly heard a deep voice yell a battle cry from the second-floor window. Thea looked up to see Charles jumping to the ground with Fig in one hand and an epic jeweled sword in the other. Fig leaped from his grasp and rushing up the dragon's spikey back while Charles charged with the beautiful weapon.

"Fig. NO!" Thea cried as her furry friend was flung to the ground by the violent twisting of the dragon. The cat howled. He backed up to the edge of the trees, never taking his eyes off of the dragon. Fig made contact with Thea in the trees. Charles, stabbing at the belly of the beast, and the dragon was launching streams of fire at the man. Thea launched another thunderbolt at the dragon, while Agatha finally conjured some water to cast too.

Sorgin launched another fire stream at Thea, who had to dive out of the way. Fig began to growl louder and louder but was no longer facing the dragon. He was instead focused behind Thea at the large shadowy creature that was behind the wall of fire. The Grimalkin had returned. Fig let out a terrifying growl that did not sound like it could come from this little cat. To Thea's amazement, Fig began to grow. His orange fur turned fiery red as he rose to the same size as the Grimalkin. With a flash of speed, Fig jumped through the wall of fire towards the shadow. "FIG!" Thea cried as she heard the two cats growl and scream in the darkness.

Thea was quickly brought back to the battle with the dragon, as a large fireball made contact with her back and ignited her clothes. She rolled in the dirt, putting out the flames, as she cried in pain. She ran as fast as she could to the bushes nearby. She saw Charles take another swipe at the dragon's underside as Sorgin was attempting to get Agatha. The beast continued to attack regardless of the underbelly that was gushing blood.

Thea saw Agatha in the jaws of the dragon. Sorgin flung the witch high into the air, then opened her mouth as if to eat her. Just as Agatha was about to land into the dragon's mouth, Thea hit the dragon in the face with a thunderbolt. Agatha fell to the ground, laid motionless on the grass. The dragon roared in pain. Thea had to act fast before Agatha got trampled. She conjured enough water to empty the lake; all of the water was built into one ample wall. She violently swung her arm towards the dragon; the wall created a tidal wave, sweeping the dragon across the yard. Agatha and Charles were also swept in the wave towards the house, crashing into a wall. Charles was still moving, but Agatha was unconscious, having slammed hard against the front entry way.

Thea quickly took her hand to the sky and brought a thunderbolt down upon the dragon's head. Sparks flew into the air as the electrical current made Sorgin shake uncontrollably. The dragon's eyes rolled back into her head as she shook and fell with a large splash. The mighty dragon had dropped but was still breathing. Charles ran towards the dragon and swung his sword across her neck. In one mighty blow, he severed the head from her body. The dragon's body changed back to her human form. Charles searched among the trees and found a branch that was still on fire, which brought to the head of Sorgin, now in human form. He picked her up by the hair and held the flame to the severed neck, cauterizing it. The smell of burning flesh turned Thea's stomach as she slowly limped out of the trees. Charles tossed Sorgin's head on top of her lifeless body and lit it all on fire.

Thea made her way to Charles, and wordlessly placed her hand on his chest as she healed the few wounds he had. She then made her way over to Agatha's motionless body lying on the front stoop. From the way her arms and legs were lying, Thea could tell that her back was broken. Thea laid her head on Agatha's chest. She could still hear a faint heartbeat. "Help me straighten her out," Thea said to Charles. They stretched her out on the lawn, her bones popping and cracking as they moved her. Thea felt the electricity run through her fingers as she saw Agatha's bones snap back into a joint. Thea was so weak from the battle that she started to pass out before she was finished with the healing. Her head swayed back and forth as she stared ahead at the burning trees. She saw a dark shadowy cat figure running towards them. "NO!" She screamed as her eyes rolled back into her head, and she fell to the ground.

Chapter Seventeen

The yard of Chateau MelBel had been destroyed, as well as the entire front of the house. Every window that had been shattered was now boarded up. The forest was burnt to nothing. A few water nymphs were seen sitting in the little water left of the lake, singing for rain.

Thea could feel the warmth of the sun on her face as she slowly started to open her eyes. She started coughing up black bile as usual. "Charles! She's waking up!" Agatha yelled out the door. She looked up to see that there was another bed in her room. Agatha was lying there with her left arm, right leg, and her entire mid-section wrapped in bandages. Her sides were in a splint to hold her spine in place.

Fig was lying on Thea's legs, his paw in a bandage; his whiskers and the tip of his ear were missing. He licked Thea's hand until she started to pet him. "I'm so glad to see you, sweet boy. I thought you got eaten." She had tears in her eyes.

"He was the cat that came out of the flames. We don't know what happened to the Grimalkin," Charles said from the door. Agatha was trying to sit up by herself when Charles came into the room. Thea's head was throbbing, and her arm was asleep from lying on her side. "I've been rolling you from side to side so that you don't get sores," He said to her with a smile. This was the first time she had ever seen him smile. His perfect teeth gleamed as he helped Thea sit up. She groaned with pain as she moved; her back was blistered and wrapped in bandages.

"How long have I been out this time?" Thea asked.

"Six days," Agatha responded in a nervous voice from her sickbed.

Thea's face turned cold when she looked at her. "Never speak to me again," she said icily. Thea flinched with pain as she tried to stand.

Charles was at her side and offered a hand. "Thank you," she said softly to him.

Agatha was quietly crying in her bed. "Thea…I….I'm so sorry. You don't understand the situation that she put me in."

Thea was livid. "You got what you wanted…whoever you are. Sorgin is dead, and you saved your sister. There is no need for you to worry yourself with anything about me, ever again." Thea was speaking very slowly and in an icy voice. She limped to the window and looked out.

Agatha was full-on bawling now.

"SHUT UP! You have nothing to be upset about!" Thea had her arms at her side, her hands in fists.

"She took my twin sister while Robin, while she was looking for you. Sorgin collects powerful…. things. She wanted a powerful witch…. and would only let her go if I brought her a stronger one, but you didn't remember. I had to make you remember." She was trying to talk in between sobs and started to hyperventilate.

"So, go get your sister, and LEAVE ME ALONE!" Thea's face was boiling as she raised her hand with a fireball up to her shoulder. Agatha stopped crying immediately and was trying to get up to run but couldn't move independently. Charles grabbed Thea's wrist and lowered the fireball. His kind eyes looked into hers. "No, Thea," he said sweetly as he squeezed her wrist lightly.

Thea let out a sigh and dissolved the fireball. "Where is your sister? Charles killed the dragon; go release her."

Charles and Agatha looked at each other with solemn looks. "The witch is dead, but her curse is not." He looked down at his wrist where the magical bracelet manacled him. "I still cannot open any of the doors that have been forbidden; I can't leave the grounds." He said, holding his wrist up. The black band was still there, digging into his skin.

Agatha said, "I found a spell that can melt the binding, but I will need a strand of unicorn hair. I know there is a unicorn out in the barn; however, Charles cannot open the door because of the band. We haven't found the man in the jumpsuit that tends to the barn."

Thea looked at them, then limped over to her bag and pulled out the shimmering strands of unicorn hair that she had got while she was riding with Eleonore. "Here." She handed it to Charles.

His face lit up like a child with a new toy. "Thank you, Miss Thea!" he said. He was about to hug her, but Thea winced in pain before he even touched her. He stopped short and carefully kissed her on her forehead. "Thank you!" He brought the hairs over to Agatha.

"I need to get to the kitchen so that I can brew this. Thea? Will you heal me so that I can move?"

Thea whipped around and glared at Agatha. "YOU DO NOT DESERVE MY HELP!" Thea screamed.

She stormed out of the room as best she could with her injuries while Fig limped behind her. Once in the hallway, Thea healed her little cat. "There you go, sweet boy."

Thea checked all the rooms on all the floors, finding that the majority were locked. The ones that weren't were either bathrooms or storage closets.

In the hallways were many cases, filled with Sorgin's collections; Thea passed cases filled with figures, thimbles, spoons, plates, cups, medals, and even one that held eyeglasses. Sorgin had collected anything she could have put her hands on.

Thea made her way up to the chateau's sixth floor and found Sorgin's bedroom at the end of the hallway. "Of course, it's locked," Thea said to Fig as she shook the handles. She tried to break the glass, but everything just bounced off the doors with a great force. Fig was exploring around the baseboards. *Could it be that simple?* Thea thought to herself. She raised her hand and ran it over the door frame: nothing, no keys to be found.

Thea ventured down to the sitting room where Charles had brought the remains of Sorgin. He had placed her body in a wooden box and had a couple of shovels sitting next to it. Thea looked inside to see the charred remains lying in a curled-up heap, just as she had landed in the yard. The severed head was carefully placed in a square glass display box, just as much of her collections had been. "That's fitting." Thea giggled as she looked at the chest. Fig jumped up on the table and was sniffing the glass. "I wonder why Charles is keeping the head here and not burying it with the body?" Thea asked out loud. Just then, Sorgin's eyes open, and the head began to scream.

Thea and Fig jumped back in fright, landing on the couch. They stared at the screaming head in wonderment. Charles came running into the room and sighed relief when he saw Sorgin screaming and not Thea.

He walked over and hit his fist on top of the glass case. "Quiet in there, or I'll cover you up again!"

The screaming immediately stopped, and Sorgin looked up at

Charles. "I want my body back," the head spoke to him.

"It's getting buried in the backyard today; you are not getting it back; you have done enough damage to all the creatures you have trapped here, in this house," he spoke calmly to her.

Thea was still staring at the talking head and Charles. "How is this possible?!" Thea asked over the bantering of the two. They stopped talking, and both looked at her. Sorgin's head started to cackle.

"She's immortal. That's why I had to cauterize her neck so that she couldn't grow her body back. She's only half-witch; her other half is an imp. That is why she's so powerful and also why she has this obsession with collecting things and making trade deals. People always end up owing her more than what they had agreed upon."

"An imp? Really? Is anyone human around here?" Charles pointed at himself, but Thea continued ranting at the severed head. "Sorgin, how do I get everyone out of their prisons you put them into?" Thea had her face down to Sorgin's eye level.

The head smiled back at her. "Prison? It's not a prison. I am keeping them safe, just as I have kept you two safe," she said as she glanced at the cat. "The Crow Witch could have easily destroyed you, or this house without me protecting it…protecting you. You see me as evil when all I was doing was protecting you from being killed." Sorgin said with a sickly-sweet smile.

"The things you have locked up in your collection don't see it that way, Sorgin; we have to let them leave. Where are your keys, and how do I break the curses on the seals?" Thea was speaking very calmly as she was talking. However, her head was pounding, and she was getting annoyed.

"She won't give the keys up. She always pulled them out of her apron when she wanted me to go somewhere and then controlled me to give them right back to her." He said as he pointed down to his wrist.

"I am stronger than you, even without my body. Death is what makes all men equal, and I cannot die. That makes me stronger than you." As Sorgin laughed, she tilted her head back as far as it would go on the little stub of her neck. Thea caught a glimpse of something shiny in her hair.

"Charles, did you see that?" Thea said as she pointed at the head.

Sorgin stopped mid-laugh and had a shocked look on her face. "See what?" Sorgin asked before Charles did.

"Does she have something in her hair?" Charles asked mischievously. He walked over to the case and lifted the glass.

"LEAVE ME ALONE! DON'T TOUCH ME!" Sorgin started to yell as she made a chomping motion towards their hands.

"Hold still. You're not so powerful without your hands, now, are you?" Charles said mockingly as he steadied the head on either side by her ears. "There you go, Thea; I've got her." Thea reached into the dirty, greasy bun of Sorgin's hair and pulled out a little copper key. The head continued to scream in protest.

"I wonder what this unlocks," Thea said to the head, as Charles was putting her back in the case.

"LEAVE MY THINGS ALONE!" Sorgin cried. "THEY ARE MY PRETTY THINGS, NOT YOURS!"

Thea examined the key, having a pretty good idea of where it would fit. "Charles, I think I am moving in the right direction today, "

"I wheeled Agatha down to the kitchen, and she is working on a brew, well, as best she can. I am going to go out back and dispose of this mess." His voice got louder at the end to ensure that the head heard him. Sorgin glared at them both from her case. "I'll make you ladies some lunch after a while."

Thea climbed the stairs to Sorgin's bedroom. The key fit and the door unlocked. There was a glimmer of blue as the spell on the door shimmered away. "Was it really that easy?" she asked Fig. The two looked at each other for a moment. She took a deep breath and held it as she pushed the doors open.

The room was gorgeous, from the canopy bed to the hand-woven rugs and the stained glass on the windows. Thea slowly walked in and started to look at all the shelves. One wall was a ceiling to floor teacups with different little flowers painted on the front. Each one had a small paper tag attached to it with a date written on it. "She did keep good records on where she got things," Thea said as she picked up a cup to examine it. Across the room, another shelf was filled with children's fairy tales from all over the world. They all were first editions and signed by the authors.
Fig went to bed and made himself comfortable. It seemed his human would be looking around this room for a while; he had already grown bored with the whole situation. Thea then found another case with thimbles inside of it. Each had a small tag with it, just like the teacups.

She walked to the stained glass window, sitting down on the built-in bench. The light in the room came from hanging lanterns that twinkled. As she looked closer to the dancing light, she realized that they were no lights at all but fairies inside of the lanterns flying in circles trying to get out.

"Oh my!" Thea exclaimed as she started to stand on the bench. She was just a hair too short of reaching them all. "I'll get all of you down," she called up to the fairies. She went back into the hallway to a closet and found a broom. She returned to Sorgin's room and used the broom handle to take each lantern down, one by one gently. She started to make a row of them across the floor. Each fairy was from a different kingdom – their wings were different shapes and colors, and the clothes they wore had other birds and flowers embellished on them. Thea couldn't make out the words that they were saying, but there was a high-pitched buzz across the room as the little fairies banged their fists on the sides of the lanterns. All together, there were twenty-three fairies in small metal lanterns sitting on the floor, each with a blue hue coming off the seals of the opening. "I'm sorry little friends, but I don't know how to get you out yet. There are more people here who are working on it."

She continued around the perimeter of the room until she got to the corner by the bed. There was a large cherry wood cabinet with the inlay of a tree in white birch. "She does have good taste," Thea said as she ran her fingers over the wood. She opened the doors and found what she was looking for: keys. Hundreds of little keys hung on hooks by different colored ribbons. Unfortunately, this was the one place where Sorgin had not labeled her collection. Thea went to the bed and removed a pillowcase and filled it full of keys. She took the heavy bag and tossed it over her shoulder with a wince of pain and was about to leave the room when the clamoring of the little fairies started up again. "I'll be back," she promised, but they weren't satisfied with that response. They got louder and started to pound harder on their lanterns. "Alright, alright! Everyone calm down." Thea said as she picked up the broomstick and ran the handle through the tops of the lanterns. She got twenty onto the broom handle and hooked the rest onto her clothing, and then hooked the pillowcase over her shoulder as she clumsily made her way out the door, with

Fig in tow.

Down the six flights of stairs, she lumbered, trying to balance the little lanterns without stepping on Fig. She made it to the main level and went into the sitting room to see Sorgin's head asleep in its case. She gently put the lanterns down on the floor in a row and then noisily dropped the bag of keys on the ground. The racket woke Sorgin from her slumber.

Sorgin's eyes opened wide in surprise as she started to scream at Thea. "DON'T TOUCH MY COLLECTION! THAT IS NOT YOURS! LEAVE MY THINGS ALONE!" The head was yelling as loud as she could.

"I think I found what you were hiding," Thea said smugly to the head. She dumped the case out on the floor. All the keys clamored to the ground.

Sorgin's screams alerted the others; Charles and Agatha came into the room. Thea looked up at the two, but the smile left her face when she saw Agatha wobble in with a cane. She couldn't help but roll her eyes whenever she saw her.

"Why is she screaming now?" Charles asked. He was covered in dirt and was cleaning his hands off with a rag.
"Look what I found," Thea scooped up a handful of keys and let them fall back into the pile.

Agatha's face lit up. "Did you find Robin?!" she exclaimed.

"No, I found hundreds of keys to open doors with," Thea coldly stated. Sorgin's head was sobbing in its case. "How do I lift the curse, you miserable little head?!" Thea yelled over the sobs.

"I think I found something," Agatha chimed in. She wobbled over to Thea and handed her a vile of sky-blue liquid. "I used up your banshee tears with the unicorn mane. I don't have enough for everyone, though." Agatha struggled to make eye contact with Thea. She looked at the bottle and then looked at the horror that was on Sorgin's face. She put a few drops onto the band strapped to Charles' wrist. It fizzed and popped, then turned into a sticky white goo as it melted off his arm. There was a blue flash of light, and it liquefied on the floor.

Charles rubbed his wrists and smiled at the girls. "You saved me!" he hugged first Agatha and then Thea. "Thank you!" He then turned his attention over to the head in the case. Thea witnessed Sorgin looking terrified for the first time since she met her. "You see now, you wicked little creature! You can't control me anymore! I am going to get my brother out of here, and then I'm going to make it, so you never see the light of day again!"

Charles started to pick up handfuls of keys and was about to head down the hallway when there was a loud ruckus coming from the front yard. He stopped and looked back at the girls. "Wait here," he said with authority.
Thea looked back at Agatha and raised her eyebrows at her. Thea wasn't going to stay put. "Let the fairies out." She gave Agatha the bottle back. Thea followed Charles to the front door. They peered out the window to see the outline of a woman standing by the lake. The Crow Witch had returned and was throwing fireballs towards the house as she cackled at the sky.

"I want my eyeball back!" Charles said, about to charge out the door. Thea grabs him by the elbow.

"Wait. Look." Thea pointed outside. The fireballs were hitting a force field about eight feet in front of the house.

Thea could hear Sorgin laughing again from the sitting room. "Do you see? How naive you are to think that I'm hurting you when I'm protecting you from her! You can leave, but then you will have to face the Crow Witch!" Her laughter filled the entire chateau as it echoed down each of the halls.

"She's right. If we leave here, we'll have to face them." Thea was looking out of the open door and could see silhouettes of ten other witches surrounding the lake.

Chapter Eighteen

Thea shut the door and headed back into the sitting room. She observed Agatha put a little drop of her blue mixture on the door to each lantern. The little fairies flew up and were ecstatic to be out of their prisons one by one. One purple fairy with golden wings flew over to Sorgin's head and spit at her. The fairies all flew over to the door quickly; they were ready to leave.

"The witches are out there," Agatha warned them as they were fluttering together.

"Yeah? There're witches in here, what's your point?!" The black-winged fairy flung his arm up, and the front door flew open. He flew out the door with purpose and left the protected area of the house. The witches by the lake used him as target practice once he got past the eight-foot mark of the front stoop. Thalia hit him head on with a thunderbolt, and he exploded into pixie dust. The rest of the fairies halted and returned to the safety of the house.

"Sorgin is just taking care of you, my sweet little collection. I don't want to hurt you; I just want to love you!" the imp head cooed to the fairies before she started to cackle again.

"I think the rest of you better stay here for a while until we figure this out," Thea said as she shut the front door.

"I only have a few drops left! We are saving them for Robin when we find her in this prison!" Agatha held the little bottle against her chest. "I made it! It's mine!"

Thea plopped down on the couch next to Fig and just stared at Agatha.

"You can barely stand, and you think you could keep that from me?" Charles said with a chuckle.

Thea started to rub her temple. "Stop," she said quietly, but the two continued to bicker at each other.

"Stop," she said a little bit louder, but they continued to poke at each other. The fairies had now started to fight amongst themselves as well; it was evident that they were all from different kingdoms and didn't seem to get along with each other.

"STOP!" Thea finally yelled at the group. The room went silent except for the snickering of Sorgin's head from her glass case. "First off, Agatha, give me some arrowroot tonic," she said with her hand out. Agatha reached into her bag and handed her a bottle. Thea took a sip of it and then looked around the room at the rest of them. "We are not going to be staying here for long, but we have to work together. We can make more of that potion, Agatha; I bet she has a banshee here or the tears of one." Sorgin's face became solemn as if she wasn't trying to give anything away. "I know there is a unicorn in the barn. We just have to find the man that tends the creatures or the right key for the barn. We will free both your brother," to Charles, "and your sister," to Agatha. "As well as everyone else in this place." She took another sip of her tonic. "Fairies…stop fighting. Can't you see she is enjoying that?" Thea asked as she motioned to the head. "We will get you out of here without being attacked by the witches outside, but you will need to help us get everyone out. There are only eleven of them. Who knows how many creatures we have in here?"

Thea got up and walked over to Agatha, and put her hands on her shoulders. She began to feel the electricity soar through her fingers as she felt the injury come out of Agatha's body and into her own. She felt light-headed and sat back down on the couch. "You don't deserve that, but I need you healthy, so you work faster." Thea glared at the lying girl.

Charles took the keys with the fairies and headed down the hall to the back door. It took almost two hours, but he finally found a key that fit the lock for the barn. Inside there were animals of all shapes and sizes with black collars around their necks. The man that Thea had seen tending to the animals wasn't a man at all but was gnome; he was inside the barn as well. Charles went over to him and let him release him first.

"What is your name?" he asked; he bent down on one knee.
"Boog," he replied softly, in a gravelly voice.

The little gnome had a scruffy beard that was full of black curly hair. He had kind eyes that changed between blue and green, depending on where he stood in the light.

"We need your help, Boog," stated Charles as they were releasing the creatures. He told the gnome how they needed unicorn hair to make a potion to lift the curse.

Boog walked over to the stall that had the unicorn in it. He patted him on the nose and spoke softly to the equestrian. "I need to pull out some of your tail so that you can go home to your family, alright?" He ran his hand up and down the muzzle of the unicorn as he spoke to him. The gnome nodded at Charles to come over as he walked around the unicorn, then pulled out ten strands of its tail. "There you are. I'll wait here until you are finished."

Charles finally took a moment to look around the barn. There was a hydra in a bin of water, as well as a mermaid. A phoenix and griffin were chained by their feet to the rafters. In the corner, a satyr played his flute. Charles just shook his head sadly at how many creatures Sorgin had tortured, tricked, and made deals with over the years.

He brought the strands of unicorn tail hair inside to Agatha in the kitchen. "Here you go!" he chimed as he continued to the sitting room. Thea was napping on the couch with Fig. She needed to recover from healing Agatha. She had placed a sheet over the case so Sorgin could not see out. The fairies were busy taking keys up and down the halls, trying them in all the locks.

A golden fairy buzzed down to the sitting room and woke Thea up. "I found one that works!" he squeaked at her. "Follow me."

She jumped off the couch, following the fairy, with Charles and Fig in tow. They went to the fourth floor, finding a room filled with bottles.

"Agatha!" Thea yelled down the hall.

A few moments later, Agatha appeared in the hallway. "Hello? Where are you?"

Thea poked her head out and waved her over. "I think you can make any spell that you want now," she said as she pushed the door open farther for Agatha to see inside.

Agatha's eyes grew wide with excitement as she saw how well the room was organized. There were eyes of newts and griffin claws, lavender, and rose oil. Everything she would ever need was in this room. "In alphabetical order even!" She exclaimed with surprise as she went straight to the banshee tears. She now had roughly thirty bottles to work with, more than enough to help everyone. She collected what she needed and headed back to the kitchen.

They worked until the wee hours of the morning, finishing the rest of the fourth floor. There were creatures from all over the realm—unfortunately, no witches or humans.

"Why did Sorgin take your brother?" Thea and Charles were busy trying keys in all the locks.

"He's the most talented warrior in all the realm. His swordplay was leaps and bounds beyond all others. He even killed a giant once."

"How did she get you?" Thea asked as she took a key out of the reject pile and tried it next door.

"I came to barter with Sorgin to get my brother released. She said that if I brought her the Emerald of Starling, she would set my brother free. I, too, am pretty good with the sword and thought for sure that I could get it. She gave me three days, and if I failed to return it to her by the sunset of the third day, I would be forced to be her servant for the rest of my days."

He continued to work on getting the door opened. "I thought it sounded like an easy enough job, as it was only guarded by one troll in Starling, and, I figured, if I failed, I just wouldn't come back. Well, when I shook her hand, she must have cast a spell on me with that black band because I failed to get past the troll, and at sunset on the third day, I was swept up in a whirlwind and ended up here. Unable to speak or do anything in the chateau I wanted unless she willed me to do so." He stopped what he was doing and looked over at her.

Thea was looking back with shock on her face. "Well, so much for that plan working," she joked at him, trying to lighten the mood, as she picked up another key.

"That was seven months ago," Charles said, shaking his head. "There are many of you who have come into this house and have never made it back out. You're lucky you were not up to par with your memory, or Agatha would have been long gone, and you would be in a jar someplace." Thea stopped and looked over at Charles.

"Why me?" she asked with a curious look on her face.

Charles chuckled before he spoke. "You are the only one not to have their soul eaten by the Grimalkin. You must be extremely strong. And she collects beautiful things if you haven't noticed." He blushed a little as he motioned around the hallway. "Two things that she looks for, all in one package. But, like everything that she collects, it has to be in mint condition. She had to fix you first before she could collect you."

A few of the rooms they had opened had brownies, trolls, even another imp. However, the search for the siblings was still unsuccessful. By the seventh day, they had made it through two floors worth of rooms. They found paintings, shoes, hats, medicine, many rooms with first edition books, and even a room full of wigs. A few of the creatures attempted to leave despite the warnings and were shot down by the witches outside. She could see Thalia and her friends through the windows. They had set up a reasonably permanent looking camp outside. They had a fire going and were roasting a pig over the coals.

The next door that she opened had perfumes in fancy glass bottles in display cases across the room. She started to sneeze immediately.

She went on to the room at the end of the hall on the first floor. She and the fairies had an assembly line system working; she sat on the floor, and different fairies would come and drop keys into her pile. She was on the eightieth key when it clicked into place.

She opened the door to find a room full of life-size dolls. All of the faces were perfectly painted, and their clothes looked of royal cloth. This was one of the largest rooms that she had found. When she saw the light, she switched it on and instantly gasped in surprise. As she had previously thought, the room wasn't filled with dolls, but people posed like dolls.

"Charles! Agatha!" she cried. Fig came running at her yells, ready to pounce. Each person had a black bracelet stuck on their wrist, just as Charles had; however, there was also a large bag that covered the whole ceiling with IVs connected to each person's arms. They were sedated. Thea walked over to someone that looked precisely like Agatha; it had to be Robin. She gazed in wonder at her porcelain skin and fiery hair. Robin's eyes moved, and Thea jumped.

"Can you move? You are Robin, right?" The girl could only blink her eyes, nothing else.

Charles and Agatha came jogging into the room, stopping in surprise. Agatha ran over to Robin, with tears in her eyes. "I knew I'd find you. I told you I would get you," she wrapped her arms around her motionless sister and cried.

Charles ran over to a guy who had on a prince's frilled shirt, with two rosy circles painted on his cheeks. "Dean. Wake up!" He shook his brother on the shoulder.

"What do you suppose the IVs are?" Thea asked.

Agatha replied, "It must be a potion to keep them like this." The girls examined the IVs and looked at each other.

A little brownie woman they had freed yesterday came in and started to unceremoniously pull the needles out of their hands. "No more spell," she said as she removed them.

Nothing happened. Everyone continued to stand motionless. Thea even tried to heal them without success. "They're not sick or injured." Agatha pointed out to Thea. "They're drugged! Hopefully, it wears off soon."

Dean looked like a darker version of Charles, with brown hair instead of blonde. Thea went over and started to wipe away the makeup on his face and realized that she had seen him before. She ripped off the shoulder of his shirt to show a small scar from an arrow wound. It was the man from the market.

"I have met your brother before," Thea said to Charles.

"Really?" he questioned as they moved the people into sitting positions.

"He's the guy with the arrow wound at the market," Agatha said as she was cleaning her sister's face.

"Arrow?" Charles asked as he walked over to his brother was standing. Thea pulled back the edge of his shirt and showed him the scar that was just below his collarbone.

There was nothing to do but wait for the potion to wear off. Sometime in the middle of the night, they started to wake up. Dean slowly opened his eyes and immediately tried to monkey flip his brother, who was patiently waiting nearby.

"Whoa! Relax, Dean; it's me," he grabbed his brother's face and forced him to look into his eyes. Charles wrapped his arms around his brother, and they hugged for a moment as if they had never thought they'd see each other again.

When Robin woke up, and immediately started to cry when she saw Agatha sitting there. "She got you too? I told you to run!" Robin was sobbing at her sister.

"It's okay, Robin. Everything is okay." she hugged her sister. Robin saw Thea over Agatha's shoulder.

"You too?!" she sobbed harder.

"No, Robin, I brought her here to help me save you. Sorgin isn't going to hurt anyone anymore." Agatha was stroking

Robin's hair to calm her down.

The others in the room were witches and humans who were the best at their trades. This included a welder and a glassblower from a kingdom in the far corner of Erresuma. The stories of how everyone got to the chateau ranged from trading a few coins to get out of tax problems, saving a member of their family, and ending up not being able to repay Sorgin. There were four witches there, including Robin. One was a shape-shifter named Riley; she could mimic the shape of any person she touched. One was a botanist named Rose, a master at making hybrid plants produce the best spells. The last was a man who could speak to animals and have them do his will. Robin, just like Thea, was supreme in training and could control all of the elements.

All of the recently freed creatures, animals, humans, and witches gathered in the chateau's sitting room to witness the severed head of Sorgin.

"She won't be harming anyone, ever again," Thea said to the group. "However, there is a new problem. There is a coven of witches who are camped out in the front of the house. They have been destroying anyone who has tried to leave." The murmur from all the side conversations grew louder as the fear of still being trapped in the chateau sounded more like a reality.

"I am protecting you from the outside world even after you turned against me," Sorgin's head cackled from under the glass case.

Thea ignored Sorgin. "These witches are strong, and we will all need to work together to get out of here and return to your families. First and foremost, those who were just rescued need to rest and get their strength back. Tonight, we rest. Tomorrow we all will have work to do. The fairies will continue to work on the doors." Thea pointed at the group of fairies flying above their heads. They all nodded in agreement. "Brownies and elves will need to split up and work with Agatha in the kitchen to make the spells and potions we might need. Dwarves and gnomes work with Charles to find weapons that we can use."

Thea was interrupted by a surly troll in the back corner of the room. "What happens if we just give you to the witches? I don't think they want anything to do with the rest of us; they will let us go if we give you to them."

Charles walked over to the troll and picked him up to eye level. "She is the reason that you are out of the bottle. I would suggest you show her some respect, mate," Charles growled at the creature.

The troll spit in Charles' face; Charles reacted by picking the troll up by the long tuft of hair growing out of the top of his head. Charles marched over to the front door. He chucked the troll out onto the lawn just beyond the end of the bubble. The witches cackled as they used the troll as target practice. "Anyone else not want to be a team player?" Charles said as he wiped his face and shut the door. The room was silent for a moment as Charles walked back into the room. Thea and the others stared in awe at the front door.

Thea cleared a lump in her throat. "I will not force anyone to help me, but please don't stand in my way of leaving here."

Charles found rooms for everyone in the house, setting them up with accommodations to be comfortable. Many of the creatures bunked with those they were locked up with for so long. They said they felt safer together.

Robin stayed with Thea and Agatha in their suite. The sisters were in the other room arguing as Thea sat looking out the window, listening to the two of them bicker. "I can't believe you brought her here like that! That's horrible of you! You didn't tell her anything, and you pretended to be me? That's the worst possible thing you could do to someone that can't remember anything!" Agatha hushed Robin, and their arguing became more of a harsh whisper on the other side of the wall. Fig joined Thea on the bench, and she scratched his ears. They both saw it at the same time! However, this time they weren't afraid of it. The Grimalkin was just beyond the edge of the trees, pacing outside the blue bubble of the force field.

Later, Robin came in to talk with Thea. "I'm sorry," Robin said. She leaned her head on Thea's shoulder; they were sitting together on the bed, staring at the painting across the room.

"You didn't do it. Your liar of a sister did. I hate her, just so you know," Thea replied. This just felt right to Thea in a way that she had never felt comfortable with Agatha- pretending to be Robin. Sitting with Robin and just talking like this felt natural and familiar. "So, do you know what I did to get everyone to want me dead?" Thea asked.

"I do," Robin said with pursed lips. "We were told that Lilly Quinn killed your parents when she was the Grimalkin, and you, in turn, were going to avenge their deaths by killing her. When you started to hunt Lilly, you found out that she was stuck as a grimalkin. Someone was controlling her, and she couldn't change back anymore." Robin was fidgeting with her hair nervously as she was telling Thea the story. "You became obsessed with finding her. All we ever did was look for her so that you could get your revenge and, so she couldn't hurt anyone else." Robin turned to look at her. "You tracked her to an area right outside of the market place. You left on your own to go after her. When the Grimalkin pounced on you, you had a fireball lit in your hand. Lilly was spitting purple fire out of her mouth as she attacked you. I tried to get to you to help, but the two of you collided, and your conjuring joined together. There was a bright flash of light. A strong force that bent the tops of the trees back and blew me to the ground. By the time

I got back to my feet, you both were gone. There was a burnt spot on the ground where you had been."

Thea had moved back to the window and was watching the Grimalkin pace around the house.

"Since that happened, the Grimalkin hasn't attacked anyone. She's been hunting you. I don't think whoever was controlling her before still has control, though. At least when people would see her before, they could call her name, and she would hesitate for a moment like she understood what was being said. Now, she just growls at everyone and runs right past them."

Thea turned to look at Robin. "So, she might not remember who she is either?" Thea questioned.

"I suppose that is a possibility. I didn't think of that. She was missing for about the same amount of time that you were. I don't know where you two went, but you were just gone."

Thea started to pace the room. "Thalia said I tried to destroy her coven?"

Robin took a breath before she started to talk. "You were a little mad. You went to the Coven, looking for Lilly before you knew she was stuck as a grimalkin. You and Thalia got into it, and between the two of you, set on fire to several of their houses, with fireballs and thunderbolts. Thalia's mother died from the smoke." Robin said quietly. "So, before you and Lilly had your flash-bang fight, you also had a coven of witches chasing after you."

Agatha chimed in from the doorway. "Remember, there are two sides to every story. You are not always the victim, even if it feels that way." With that, Agatha turned and walked back into her room.

"I may feed your sister to the Grimalkin before all of this is through," Thea said vindictively.

In the morning, all the witches met in the kitchen and were making breakfast for the hundreds of creatures living in the chateau.

"We're running out of food," the male witch, who went by the name of Devin, stated as he pulled the bread from the pantry.

"Well, we should probably not plan on staying here much longer then," Charles said, as he brought in apples from the garden.

"After we eat, we can go over the plan," Thea said as she snacked on some grapes. "The Grimalkin is out back now; we are surrounded."

Thea went over the plan with the entire group. Sorgin taunted them: "That is a coven of supremes! The whole family is filled with supremes. You think you're going to take on eleven witches and a grimalkin?!" Sorgin was laughing hysterically. "You're going to need more help than you have in this room!"

Thea started to talk over Sorgin. "Do not listen to her! We can all get out of here! You all have your assignments; meet back here at dusk." The room was disbursed except for the twins, Dean, Charles, and Thea. Fig was sitting on the table, licking the glass to Sorgin's case.

The sisters talked about getting their spells together while the boys were talking about finding weapons to use.

"Sorgin, I want to make a deal," Thea said to the head. She attempted to keep her statement hushed.

"What?! NO!" Robin and Agatha yelled at her. The boys had

stopped talking and looked at her with concern. "Thea, you don't want to do that. There is always a catch that works out in her favor."

Thea held her hand up to hush everyone. "She's right; there are only a few of each kind of creature here, not enough for them to overpower a group of supremes." Thea was staring into Sorgin in the eyes. Sorgin had a broad smile on her face. "Sorgin, if I give you your body back, will you help us with the coven?" The head smirked back at the group.

"I'll protect you all, just as I have been doing all along."

"Go get her body," Thea said with a sigh.

Chapter Nineteen

The body of Sorgin was exhumed from the backyard. A few of the dwarfs helped carry the box into the sitting room, unbeknownst to them of what it contained. Thea shut the doors to the sitting room, then took the lid off the box, preparing herself for its gruesome contents. The body hadn't decomposed at all; in fact, it looked better than it did when it was buried.

"Here's the deal, Sorgin, I will attach your head back to your body and heal you. In exchange, you will help everyone escape the Coven and the Grimalkin. AND, you can no longer collect ANY living creatures, ever again. Deal?" Sorgin was listening intensely as Thea went over their deal.

"I will continue to protect you, and I will not collect anything.... Living," the old witch replied with a sneer. Thea supposed that was the best deal she was going to get.

Thea removed the glass case, cut into the head's base, and then set the head onto the stump of the neck. There was a trickle of blood that came out of Sorgin's neck. Agatha took out a needle and thread and sewed the skin back together. Sorgin moaned with each stitch going through her crispy skin. Thea took a deep breath and placed her hands on the charred remains and started to heal the body of the immortal witch. The electric current ran through her into Sorgin. The old witch cackled as the bones in her neck started to fuse back together with her back. The skin on her neck began to grow over the stitches that Agatha placed. Her body lifted out of the box as her skin started to turn back to a healthy hue, instead of the burnt crisp, it was a few moments before. As Thea removed her hand from Sorgin, the old witch smiled as she raised her hands to smooth her hair down.

"How is that possible? Isn't she dead?" Dean whispered to

Agatha.

"She's immortal. If her head doesn't die, she can rejuvenate her own body, if she can get her head over to the body, that is," Agatha whispered back as she watched the spectacle in awe. "She's like a cockroach; she won't die."

"That feels better," Sorgin said as she stood up. "Now, let's get this over with." Sorgin put her hand on her arm where her cane had transformed into a band and pulled it off while it magically stretched back to its original state. Thea and the others wasted no time; they planned the witches' attack outside and started preparing for a battle.

Dusk was falling. All the creatures took their places throughout the chateau. The elves were in the windows with their arrows ready to fire down onto the grounds. The dwarfs stood at the door and on the porch with their sharpened axes; Charles and Dean drew their swords, ready to battle.

"Are you ready?" Robin whispered to Thea. With a deep breath, Thea nodded. "You have your necklace ready?" Robin asked as she handed Thea a small dagger. Thea nodded again as she dipped the blade into the little bottle that she had gotten from the elves, stabbing it first into her arm, then into the arms of each of the twins in turn.

"I hope Agatha's enchantment works. I don't want to have to run around naked." Thea said as they started to shrink.

"It will work!" Agatha hissed back.

As they started to shrink, they each poured more of the potion into their wounds. They shrank down to the size of ants. Riley, the shape-shifter, stood in the doorway looking just like Thea. She opened the door and walked out onto the porch.

"Thalia, this has gone on long enough! You need to leave the property!" the fake Thea shouted out to the camp. In response, each hand in the Coven slowly started to glow in the darkness with their thunderbolts ready to strike.

Meanwhile, Thea and the twins rode the back of Fig, who ran through the grass, coming up behind the witches. Mud trolls were sent covertly from the tiny girls to form a wall between the lake and the Coven. Robin sent a wave neatly over the border from the lake that extinguished the row of thunderbolts. Just then, a mighty roar came from the sitting room of the chateau as Sorgin charged out of the house in all of her dragon glory. The noise took many of the creatures by surprise, fled to the woods when they saw that Sorgin was back. The two humans locked up with Dean, made it to the edge of the trees before being buried alive by two mud trolls, which was conjured by a purple-haired witch from the Coven. The brownies and nymphs were nowhere to be seen.

The elves began to shoot their arrows from the windows, and fairies were shooting beams of light across the yard. Devin had called upon the animals from the forest to join their battle. Boog had brought the phoenix and the griffin through the house; they too joined in the attack.

Thea and the twins started to grow large again as the spell wore off. The Coven was unaware that they were now the ones who were surrounded. The three witches spread out behind the crescent shape stance of the Coven. Agatha brought forth an army of mud trolls that lined up behind each witch, while Thea and Robin had fireballs in each hand. They all released their conjuring at the same time. Sorgin swooped down in front of the group and sprayed a stream of fire in front of the witches. Charles and Dean were on either side of the massive dragon, swords drawn and waiting to move through the wall of fire. The fifteen fairies that were left were dive-bombing the witches, along with the ravens; their fairy dust bombs were hitting the witches on the heads and disorientating them.

The pale witch who had joined Thalia during their first battle had turned around and was in a physical fight with Agatha. The witch had her hand around Agatha's neck and was lifting her off the ground. Agatha was barely touching the ground with her tiptoes and was gasping for air. She dropped her hand to her waistband and removed a potion bottle that she had tied to her belt. The bottle hit the ground and shattered, emitting a yellow gas into the air that created enough of a diversion that Agatha was able to knee the witch in her throat and escaped her grasp.

Sorgin took most of the Coven hits but was now receiving back up from Rose, Riley, and Dean as they, too, were throwing homemade bombs of potions and gravel into the Coven. Charles and Dean had broken through the wall of fire, and one of them managed to decapitate a witch. Her head rolled across the grass and landed at Thea's feet. Thea awkwardly punted the head away from her as it landed in front of Thalia. She became enraged at the sight of the head staring up at her and started to scream her high-pitched screech, which caused many of the creatures to fall over and clench their ears.

"I'M GOING TO KILL YOU!" she screamed as she came towards Thea. The entire Coven began to ignore the group coming from the chateau, as one witch created a force field between Sorgin and them. Her hands were raised high above her head, and she was straining to push the bubble of energy back towards the house. She was forcefully moving the creatures around towards the chateau.

"Do it now!" Thea yelled as Robin threw the water from the lake onto the nine witches.

Thea ripped off her necklace, stabbing her dagger into the red jewel. It gave off an icy wind that froze everything went into a crystal of ice.

"NOOOOOO!" Thalia screamed. She threw one more thunderbolt before freezing solid into a statue fit for the Ice King. Electricity soared through Thea as the thunderbolt hit her, and Thea fell to the ground. Screams that could curdle blood escaped her throat as she shook uncontrollably on the wet grass.

The witch pushing the group back with her force field was distracted by a noise behind her. She turned to see her frozen sisters. At that moment, her bubble weakened, and Charles and Dean were able to push through. Dean swung his sword and cut off the burned witches' hands and flung them up into the air where Sorgin ate them in a mighty gulp.

Robin and Agatha were hovering over Thea; she was no longer moving on her own.

"Wake up, Thea, wake up!" Agatha said, running a bottle of a potion under Thea's nose. Dean came running over to her and knelt at her side. He lifted her off the ground and pressed his lips to hers and filled her lungs with his breath. The few fairies that were still left came over and sprinkled their fairy dust over Thea's body. Silvery glitter made her body shine in the moonlight.

"Open her mouth!" Agatha said as she removed another bottle from her belt and poured it down Thea's throat.

Nothing was working. She was no longer breathing on her own.
The phoenix flew down, landing on the shoulder of Sorgin, who had now taken her human form once again.

"Go on now, help her," Sorgin said to the bird as she stroked the bird under the chin. He hopped down to sit on the shoulder of Dean as a single tear rolled out of the corner of its eye and landed in Thea's open mouth. A golden wave of power glided over her skin and was soaked into her body. For a brief second, you could see her heart shine through her shirt, as it started to beat regularly on its own. She coughed and opened her eyes.

"What happened?" Thea questioned as she looked up into Dean's eyes.

"You died," Sorgin answered with the sound of amusement in her voice.

"She wasn't dead; her heart was still beating," Robin said as she scolded Sorgin. The old imp witch shrugged her shoulders, turned around, and walked back towards the house.

The witches didn't stay frozen for long; they were starting to melt—the handless was being held at bay by Charles' sword against her neck.

"Sorgin, we will need some binding bands," Robin said with authority.

"I cannot break the deal; I'm not allowed to collect living things," Sorgin said in response.

"I'm collecting them, not you!" Robin shouted at the witch's back.

Sorgin returned quickly to the group of witches. Her face lit up as she applied a black band to the ankle of the handless witch. "Now, even if her hands grow back, she won't be able to cast a spell."

Thea looked around the yard to see the disastrous aftermath of the battle that had happened. Devin was dead, lying in the grass with a few of the woodland critters sitting around him. Riley was severely injured, and Thea took to healing her the best that she could; Rose was nowhere to be found; Agatha stated that she saw her flee during the battle. Most of the creatures who were once trapped at the chateau took the opportunity to leave during the battle. Thea did her best to heal everyone that was still alive in the yard, but many did not make it. Thea was weak and having problems breathing.

"What are you doing?!" Agatha snapped at Charles, who was hacking away at the ice of Thalia's ice sculpture.

"I want my eye back! She stole it from me!" He was taking swings with his great sword, and shards of ice were falling to the ground.

"Wait! I have something better for you!" Robin went over to Thea's bag and removed the little glass bottle that had Thalia's eyeball in it. "An eye for an eye." She walked over to Charles and pulled out a small dagger. She stabbed him in the face where his eye used to be.

"What are you doing?!" he screamed as the blood started to stream down his face.

"Hold still!" she growled back at him as she placed the green eye into his head.

"Thea, heal him," she commanded, wiping her bloody hands onto her skirt. Thea walked over, placing her hand over his bloodied socket, and sent her energy soaring through her fingertips and into his face. The skin started to heal around his eye. The blood rolled up his cheek and back into his head. He now had one blue eye and one green.

"Can you see?" Dean asked softly.

"Yes!" Charles cheered as he hugged Thea.

"I need to rest," Thea said as she started to walk back to the house. Sorgin had a few gremlins and gnomes that hadn't left to move the frozen witches into the house to one of her collection rooms. The handless which was healed by Thea but couldn't cast any spells because of Sorgin's binding. She was also locked into one of Sorgin's many rooms.

Thea looked around the yard one more time and saw her friends there, walking back in a group to the house. Robin, Agatha, Riley, Charles, and Dean. She smiled at them and breathed a sigh of relief, but then paused for a moment as she looked down to the ground.
"Where's Fig? Where is my cat?!" she yelled in a panic. "Has anyone seen Fig?"

Chapter Twenty

Panicky and barely able to move, Thea dragged herself through the house, yelling for her cat the whole way.

"Fig?! Where are you?! FIG!!!!???" she screamed for her little orange cat.

Where is he?! What happened to him?!

The few elves that stayed behind shook their heads no when asked if they had seen the cat. Thea made her way out to the backyard to where Boog was with the creatures that were left. She could see the baby bear past the force field of the yard; he was lying in a heap with a massive bite taken out of his side.

"Have you seen my cat!?" she frantically asked Boog. He pointed towards the barn.

"Meow," she heard a faint cry from the long grass by the barn.

"Fig?" She ran over to the barn.

"He attacked the Grimalkin, while protecting the creatures that were trying to leave. The Grimalkin was here for a moment until there was that loud scream of a banshee-then, she was gone," Boog stated in a low voice as he touched Thea gently on the shoulder.

Fig laid on his side, with his fur soaked in blood. He no longer looked orange, but a red lump of fur, caked in mud. He could barely lift his head to look at his human.

Thea put her hands on her little cat and healed his cuts, as tears of relief rolled down her face. She sat down in a heap and leaned against the barn. She hacked up the bile brewing in her stomach and shut her eyes. She could see the earth spinning and felt every movement of every being around her. She couldn't move, couldn't speak, but had an overwhelming sense of everything happening around her.

I can hear you, little cricket. I just can't make it over to you. Did I help enough? Did I help at all? Is Fig alright? He has to be....right? Move body! Move!

Am I alright? Can they hear me? Guys?

Thea looked around wildly with her eyes but couldn't control the movement of her body anymore. Her friends had noticed her and detoured from the house to help.

"Let's get her to her bed," Dean said.

She could feel her body floating up in the air. She must have been carried back to the house. She couldn't move nor open her eyes, but she couldn't sleep either. She was trapped within herself in a comatose state. She could hear the words but couldn't separate the voices.

Who was talking?

"How did she know how to do that? How did she know her necklace had powers?"

"She must have read about it in her book."

"Sorgin could have told her. She wanted the necklace."

"Who is the Ice King?"

"I think she knew how from her spell book she has been carrying around. But she said someone left her notes? Who did that?"

"What are we going to do with the Coven? Do we kill them?"

"We can't kill them! We're not murderers…..are we?"

"Will they stay with Sorgin? That doesn't sound very smart to me. That sounds like giving an evil army to a witch imp."

"What are we going to do about the Grimalkin?"

"Did you see how fast all those creatures took off once the fight broke out? There was no loyalty for freeing them."

The voices started to fade into the darkness that surrounded Thea. She fell into a sleep filled with flashes of the battlefield, and the screams of Thalia echoed in her head.

"Thea is waking up!" Robin called down the hallway. Thea opened her eyes and saw that she was in a different room than she had stayed in before. Robin handed her a glass of water.

"Thanks," she said in a cracking voice. Fig was there at her side, watching her every move. "Hi, sweet baby," she said as she smiled down at her cat, starting to cry. "I thought I was too late." She drank her water too fast and started to choke on it; Thea coughed up more black bile into the bin by the side of the bed.

"What happened with the ice cubed witches?" Thea said, with a moan as she tried slowly getting out of bed. Dean was there to help her to her feet. He held her tight to his side as he supported her; she shut her eyes as she breathed in his scent. Her legs still felt weak, but she knew that they had to finish this adventure.

"You'll have to come to look," Robin said as she nodded towards the door. The group headed down the hallway and took a flight of stairs down to the basement. In the back corner, there was a little door that was no higher than Thea's knee. The large room was dimly lit by a flickering light bulb. The room felt cool, and the dampness was apparent by the condensation on the walls. The basement was filled with old crates that were stacked up to the ceiling. Old rugs of different colors made a patchwork on the cement floor.

"They're in there," Charles said, pointing to the little door. Agatha dropped to her knees. She turned the latch with a rusty squeal from the hinge, opened the door. Thea peered in to see that the door was high above a pit. There sat the Coven, frozen from the neck down, with bracelets binding their wrists. The room was covered in enchanted ice and snow, ensuring that the witches stayed frozen.

"How did you guys do that?" Thea whispered back to the group. "There're no stairs leading down there."

"There were some stairs, but we burned them down once they were in there. There was a little magic left in your necklace that we used to make a spell to keep it in a permanent freeze. They shouldn't be getting out of there," Agatha said with a nod. She gave one last glance into the icy room below as she blew her clouded breath out. "Each of them has one of Sorgin's bands attached to them. Even if the ice melts, they are not able to cast spells. Sorgin must have attached them while we were looking for Fig."

Thea stared down into the room for a moment longer before she shut the door and turned the key. "And, what did you guys do about Sorgin?" she questioned, as she slowly stood up with the help of Dean. She smiled softly at him as she leaned on his arm.

"She disappeared when we went looking for Fig," Dean said with a grim look on his face. Thea looked up into his eyes and sighed deeply. She wasn't ready to deal with that problem.

Charles led them back upstairs to the kitchen and fixed them some dandelion fizzy and a bowl of pasta to eat. As they sat around the table and had their lunch, their spirits were lifted now that the Coven had been defeated.

"How long have I been out?" Thea asked as she smoothed her greasy hair down with a feeling of disgust.

"Nineteen days," Robin responded, with a look of concern. "You will still need to rest." Thea nodded as she realized how tired she felt.

"What's the plan now?" Agatha asked Thea; clearly, the group had been waiting for her direction. Thea looked up to meet her eyes.

"What do you mean, 'the plan'?" Thea questioned her, making air quotes with her fingers and giving Agatha an annoyed look.

"Yeah, what are we doing?" Agatha asked her. She looked at Thea with wide eyes as she waited for an answer. Everyone else looked back and forth between the two, awkwardly, not wanting to make eye contact with either one of them.

"I am going to go find the Grimalkin… and you are going to go about your life," Thea responded with a death stare. The others in the group fidgeted in their seats and poked at their lunches. Robin started to cough as she choked on her fizzy drink.

"Sorry," Robin said as she cleared her throat. "We're all coming with you, Thea. You're not strong enough to do anything on your own yet. You need to let go of your anger with Agatha. She was only-"

"She was only trying to give me to a psychotic witch-imp to be turned into a life-size doll. I owe her nothing, and I don't want to be associated with her! I should have left her on the front lawn when Sorgin tried to eat her!" Thea quickly shot Agatha a look down to the end of the table that would have frozen anyone in their tracks. "I need to finish what I started and try to remember the passion that started this quest. You guys all remember your childhood and your families. I don't." She was becoming agitated with this conversation, and the expression on her face was more than enough to show the drive burning behind her eyes. If Thea had been able to walk on her own, she would have stormed off.

"Thea, without you, none of us would be able to leave this house, and we would still be sitting up in that room, staring off in a timeless daze." Dean reached out a hand and touched her arm as he spoke. "You have saved me twice, and I am going to be there to help you in every way I can. Robin and Charles are in the same boat….and if Agatha didn't bring you here, none of that may have happened. It's like you say…. there're two sides to each story, right?" Charles nodded his head in agreement with what Dean was saying. He looked down at the drink in his hand. Robin was watching Agatha with sorrow in her eyes.

"We're all going with you," Charles added to the conversation with authority in his voice. "There is no reason to fight it."

Thea let out a sigh; she just nodded her head as she pushed her food around with her fork. "Fine." was all she offered as an answer. She slid her plate away from her on the table and used all her arm strength to push herself up to a standing position, to leave the room. "I need to rest. I'm leaving tomorrow, with or without all of you." She went back to her room, leaning on Dean's arm, with her little fluffy cat in tow. She could hear the group's muffled conversation back at the table but didn't care about what they were saying. All she wanted to do was be done with all of this.

The next morning, Thea and Fig got out of bed before the sun was up. Charles had breakfast waiting on the table for her, just like he had back when Sorgin was in control. She sat at the table and ate the cheese and fruit that he had left for her and a short stack of pancakes with boysenberry syrup.

"Well, Fig, I think it's time to go hunting. Are you ready?" The cat got up and walked over to the door and started to scratch at the wood. Thea smiled and collected her things as she readied herself for the next chapter of her adventure.

She made her way towards the front door but stopped when she reached the bottom step. Charles, Dean, and the twins were sitting in front of the door with their things packed. The girls had their bags full of herbs and a couple of books, while Charles was sharpening a massive sword and Dean was twirling the top of an ax onto a fresh handle. Fig trotted over to the group and joined them in the huddle on the floor.

"Are you ready?" Robin asked Thea in a chipper tone to her voice. Thea looked back at the group in shock. She just shook her head in disbelief as she led the group outside. "You didn't think you were going to leave us behind, did you?"

But she had thought that the others were bluffing, and she was going to leave them behind. She couldn't wrap her head around all of the support that they were offering her. Why would they want to help her when so far, she had only caused death and destruction at every turn?

"The gnomes said they would feed the witches and take care of the few creatures that have stuck around. We cleared out the majority of the food that would keep while we traveled." Agatha told Thea. "So, where would you like to start?"

"We should go out back and track the Grimalkin's path from the barn, as that was the last place that we know her whereabouts," Charles suggested.

"That makes sense," agreed Thea; she walked around the side of the chateau. "Let's get going."

The group said goodbye to Boog and gave him all of the keys to the chateau, with instructions to keep the witches locked up and to feed the few creatures and critters that were still on site. He was happy to be in charge of the large building. He kept referring to himself as the Key Master, with an enthusiastic smile.

Charles and Dean led the way as they followed the tracks to the south of the chateau. The trek was long, and it took them a few uneventful days before they were out of the trees. They entered into a grassy field that stretched as far as they could see. The sweet smell of the flowers made Thea feel sleepy as they pushed through the marshy ground.

They were four days into the journey, and they still had not seen a sign of the Grimalkin; the massive cat-like footprints always seemed to be a day old when they found one, regardless of how fast they were traveling. There were some cottages here and there, and at the end of the grassy field, there was the dirt road that leads into Owl's Nest, the town where the twins had grown up many years ago.

"The footprints are headed right into the town," Charles said, on bended knee, examining the dried mud on the road. "I don't have a good feeling about that at all."

"Hopefully, she just passed through," Agatha chirped, trying to be optimistic for the group.

"Yeah, she's done a really good job of just 'passing through' places," Thea said sarcastically as she continued down the road. "Let's go see what damage she's done."

"You don't have to be so mean to her, Thea. She's sorry for what she did. You need to let go and forgive her," Robin whispered over Thea's shoulder, catching up to her.

"I forgave her a long time ago. It doesn't mean I have to forget what happened." Thea gave Robin a sideways glance as they were whispering. "I have a feeling in the pit of my gut that I shouldn't trust her. I had that feeling since I met her, and I didn't listen to it." Thea trailed off, shaking her head in frustration.

The boys were far ahead, playfully tracking the Grimalkin. They acted like twelve-year-olds whenever they thought no one was paying attention to them. Thea giggled to herself and thought about how happy she was around Dean. Agatha was between the girls and the boys, pulling her wagon and talking to Fig, who was hitching a ride.

The closer they got to Owl's Nest, Thea started to notice an unusual number of ravens and sparrows following across the field. Once they reached the next section of the forest, there were hundreds of them on the branches.

"I think your friends are here, Thea," Robin said over the squawking of the birds. Thea looked up to see the birds all looking down upon them from the branches. Thea recognized one of the large dark ravens that had been with them at the market. He had a bit of purple string hanging from his mouth. He called out when he made eye contact with Thea. Black wings delicately fluttered down to Thea's shoulder, and he cautiously dropped something for Thea to pick up.

"What did you bring me, my little friend?" Thea asked as she bent down and picked up the piece of ribbon. There was a small bronze key attached at the end of the cord. "Interesting," she commented, holding it up for the group to see. The massive bird then flew up to the top of Thea's staff and perched there. "I guess you're coming along too," she said to her bird with a wink.

"You and your key collection," Agatha said as she looked at the key. "What does this one open?" Thea shrugged her shoulders.

"I haven't a clue, but if I have learned anything from this adventure, it's to hang onto keys." With that statement, she pulled out her stash of keys and tied the string to the other keys.

They made their way to the center of the square, where the tracks traveled around the central fountain, then off in different paths between the buildings. The houses were painted with bright, cheery colors, had window boxes with petunias planted in them, and little straw doormats on each threshold, yet it was eerily quiet throughout the streets.

"I don't think she just passed through here, Agatha," Thea said as she looked around the town. The birds had followed them in through the trees and were perched on the straw roofs. Fig was sniffing the ground around the fountain and following the girls as they wandered about.

"Do we start knocking on doors?" Dean questioned as they were peering around houses. "There doesn't seem to be much movement around here."

"I think we should keep going. I don't think the Grimalkin is going to answer the door." Robin said as she was looking at the paths and kicking stones. "How do the tracks go off in two different directions?" She pointed both towards the east and the west of the town.

"We should split up and see where they lead," Charles suggested sitting on the edge of the fountain. "The sun is high in the sky; we should each go for two hours and then report back here." The group all looked at him.

"You want to split up and go find the Grimalkin? That sounds horrible. Someone is going to get eaten," Thea responded. She started off towards the east, where the tracks were deeper than the rest. "I'm going to head this way. You all should follow me if you want to stay together. I think it is just plain stupid to split up."

"There are tracks going in both directions. We need to see where they lead. More will get accomplished if we split up," Dean spoke calmly, trying to persuade Thea into the separation.

"My head is hurting, so I'm not going to argue with you. I'm headed east. You guys do what you want." Thea headed towards one set of tracks with her little orange cat right behind her. Robin slowly looked at the faces of her friends, and then solemnly walked with Thea without saying a word.
"How about you and Agatha head to the west, and I will go with these two towards the east? Then we will cover both sets of tracks. Go two hours out, and then return to the fountain." Dean was watching the upper windows as he spoke and saw the faces of the town's people peeking out from behind their curtains. Their eyes were full of fear when Dean met their gaze. He nodded at a few of them. "These people will feel better once we track her down." Charles nodded and shook his brother's hand.

Dean, Robin, and Thea walked towards the east, following the set of tracks that went into the thicket of trees. The group was pretty quiet for the most part as they went on their way. The large raven squawked every few steps with annoyance for the bumpy ride on Thea's walking stick but didn't fly away.

The tracks continued to head east for a while but then circled back to the west, where they had begun. They backtracked the ground they had already covered and passed the village.

"We still have a half-hour before we are to meet at the village; I think we should keep going since we're headed towards them anyway," Thea said as she knelt down to look at the tracks on the ground. Fig stopped and sniffed the massive footprint and hissed.

"Let's keep moving then," Dean said as he offered Thea a hand up.

They walked to the top of a grassy hill. There was an open valley between the trees that looked to be a dried lakebed. There were about a hundred creatures and humans walking in circles down in the valley. None of them made a noise. They would sometimes walk into each other, bouncing off, then changing directions. Robin raised her eyebrows and looked back at the others with a befuddled look on her face.

"What is going on there?" Dean questioned the witches.

"I'm not sure..." Thea said slowly as her voice trailed off.

What's going on? Why are there fairies and elves walking about with the humans?

What happened to all of them? Where is the Grimalkin?

"They don't look to be well," Robin said as she cautiously followed Thea over the hill. The three of them, and the little orange cat, headed down the path to the wandering bodies. Each one had a blank stare on their face as they aimlessly walked amongst the crowd. Dean, Thea, and Robin walked alongside them, trying to get their attention, but there was no recognition from the blank faced people. They would get bumped into, and then the person would just walk away.

"Hello?" Thea said as she waved her arms in front of the face of a woman walking towards her. "Can you see me?" The woman kept walking forward and bumped into Thea. The woman took a step back and started to walk in a different direction. Thea looked over her shoulder at Dean with confusion.

"They've all been….stupefied," Dean said, as he tried to shake a slender man by his shoulders. The man stood still while being held, but when Dean stopped shaking the man, he just changed directions.

"Do you see their eyes?" Robin asked as she was studying a portly woman walking next to her. "The iris' are all purple. How many people do you know with purple eyes?"

Thea looked into the eyes of many of the creatures and people walking by. Sure enough, each of them had purple eyes that were staring off in the distance as they walked aimlessly.

"Hey! Come on! We got to go! What is wrong with you?!" they suddenly heard Agatha's voice shrieking on the other end of the valley.

"Is that your sister?" Thea said in a hushed tone of annoyance, not knowing if that was friend or foe yelling across the way.

"It sounded like her," Robin said, as she stood on her tiptoes trying to see over the sea of people.

"I see her red hair over there," Dean said as he pointed across the way.

The group made their way over to where they heard the yelling, bouncing off the stupefied people and tripping over little gnomes and trolls along the way.

"Agatha? Where are you?" Robin yelled out, still trying to see over the people.

"Robin? I'm over here!" Agatha's small frame started bouncing up and down to be seen by the group.

Agatha ran to the group in hysterics. Charles was being dragged by his arm behind Agatha as she made her way over to them. "We found the Grimalkin!" she cried, falling into her sister's arms. "Charles attempted to fight it, but it did this to him!" Agatha tugged on his arm and whipped him around to face the others. His eyes were the same violet hue that all the other creatures had. "The Grimalkin took his soul! It wrapped its arms around Charles, and there was all of this smelly smoke, and then he was like this!" Agatha was now sobbing uncontrollably.

Dean grasped Charles by his upper arms and stared into his eyes; he was too upset to speak.

"Smelly?" Robin asked as she pushed her sister away from their embrace to look at her face.

"It smelled like sulfur," Agatha said with a sniffle, wiping her face with her sleeve.

"Sulfur?" Thea repeated in a confused tone. "That sounds more like a spell than anything else." She jogged back to the cart and started to dig through the books there. Agatha nervously looked around the stupefied group. Thea thumbed through her book and found the page she was looking for. "Here!" she yelled out to the others as they made their way to her.

"What did you find?" Dean was pushing his way through the herd of people to where Thea was standing; he now had his brother over his shoulder, which was made difficult due to Charles' continuously moving legs.

"It is a spell! These people haven't had their souls eaten; they are all just in a trance. Thea handed the book to Robin to review.

"We should be able to reverse this if we find the witch that cast it or the right antidote." Robin was speaking slowly as she read over the book.

"No! It was the Grimalkin! I know what I saw!" Agatha chimed in. She was looking between the girls, desperately hoping to get one of them to believe her.

"That may be well and good, Agatha, but I'm telling you that these people have a spell on them; their souls are intact. They don't look like any of the Grimalkin victims that people have described.

They continued to debate between the options of the Grimalkin eating people's souls, and it is a spell when they were interrupted by an explosion off in the woods. Smoke and bright light were rising above the trees. Birds started to squawk and fly away from the area as fast as their wings would take them. A witch's cackle echoed from that direction.

"I think we better go towards that," Thea said with a frightened look on her face. "Someone, or something, is trying to get our attention."

"What about these people? And Charles?" Agatha asked with concern as she was looking into Charles' blank, violet eyes.

"They all seem to be just fine here; we will come back for

them," Dean set Charles down on the ground, and he immediately got up and started to aimlessly walk in circles with the rest of the creatures. Dean drew his sword and started to walk back up the path towards the smoldering ash that was now raining down on the field.

"He'll be okay here," Robin said, as to comfort Agatha while she gently led her towards the path.

The group headed towards the smoky haze rising above the treetops. They weren't alone. There were many creatures moving through the trees towards the fire. They slowly crept out of the darkness of the forest to where the fire was brightly burning. Thea saw many of the same creatures that were trapped in Sorgin's prison, now walking with spears, bows, and swords. The Grimalkin's dark shadowy presence engulfed the clearing, with her yellow eyes glowing. She looked at everyone who was gathered there. The ravens and sparrows had finally stopped squawking in the trees; the eerie silence made Thea feel uneasy as she twisted her staff in her hands. The air turned cold as the Grimalkin moved closer to the girl. Fairies, elves, and humans alike raised their weapons, ready to attack.

Thea dropped her staff where she stood. Her raven friend flew up to the trees. Thea raised her hand out at her side. She drew all the fire from the pit to her hand. The flames swirled in orange and yellow and nestled restlessly in her palm, creating a massive fireball that was larger than Thea's head. The Grimalkin roared; the force of its breath pushed the spectators back into the trees. The mighty cat lowered its head and charged towards Thea. The beast opened its mouth and disbursed an ample violet flame. Thea charged towards the fire and threw her own flame towards the creature.

Red and violet flames engulfed the Grimalkin and Thea. Their bodies rose off the ground and went flying straight up into the branches of the trees before crashing back to the ground at an accelerated speed. The explosion of light that followed was brighter than the sun. It temporarily blinded everyone in the area; The noise was a deafening, high pitched squeal. Robin fell to her knees, covered her ears, and screamed, though no one could hear her. Her eardrums had ruptured upon the impact. The tops of the trees around the fire had ignited, casting shadows against the night sky; The creatures retreated to the dark corners of the forest. The air was scented with the smell of burning flesh, and the smoke was a thick, smog-like blanket that covered the entire clearing in the forest.

When the ringing in their ears had subsided, Dean helped Robin to her feet, while Agatha fanned the faint haze from in front of her face. Fig ran over to a large lump on the ground and was meowing to the group.

"Thea!" Dean yelled as he ran over and held her head up off the ground. "Can you hear me? Are you okay?" He lightly shook her shoulders as he slid his body under hers to support her better. The green of her eyes sparkled intensely as she opened them. She let out a sigh and then started to cough from the smoky air.

"Did I get her? Did it work?" Thea said as she struggled to get out of Dean's lap.

"Look over there!" Robin exclaimed as she pointed to an ample dark mass in the shadows of the fire that was slowly stirring on the other side of the clearing. Dean drew his sword while Agatha and Robin each had thunderbolts ready to throw; Thea had a fireball in each hand as they marched into the hazy darkness. Fig had grown into a massive cat and was prepared to pounce.

The Grimalkin moaned and took deep, slow breaths.
"You're done hurting people, Lilly! This is the end!" Thea and the twins raised their spells high above their heads and, with a

nod, released them at the Grimalkin. Thunderbolts struck the ground rhythmically as the fire soared through the center of its massive body. Dean then lunged towards the Grimalkin, running his sword through the middle of the dark figure. Fig pounced on the figure, grabbed it by the jugular, and shook the mighty beast until it went limp.

The sky opened, and the darkness lifted. The birds started to slowly come back, and the deafening silence was no longer ringing through their ears. Thea looked down at the Grimalkin, took in a deep breath, and slowly let it out. Fig came over and sat by her leg, calmly cleaning his muzzle with his paws. Thea looked back at the faces of her friends; their hair was a frizzy mess, and there was black soot smeared across their faces. Thea wiped her own face as she walked over to the limp body of the Grimalkin. She drew out Dean's sword and then poked the leg; it didn't move. She lifted the sword with both hands over her head and started to swing down towards the neck of the beast when the Grimalkin suddenly lifted its head and started to laugh like an old woman.

The laughter made Thea jump; she was in mid-swing and brought the sword down to the ground, missing her intended target. The Grimalkin transformed into a small woman. Her skin was wrinkled, and her hair touched the ground in wiry, gray masses. Her eyes were the darkest of browns that looked completely black, so you couldn't even see the pupils. She wore a cloak of emerald green, which sparkled in the firelight. Her laugh was cracked and high pitched. She didn't look anything like the stories depicted her. She wasn't long or lean; she didn't have any features of an elf. She looked more like a small imp woman, like Sorgin.

"Lilly?" Thea asked as she pulled the sword back to strike the old woman.

"Lilly? Lilly? Oh, Lilly Quinn, where can she be?" the old

woman sang back to Thea, as she pointed a long finger towards Thea's face. "You can't remember what happened to Lilly, silly. How many grimalkins can there be?" With that, the old woman started to laugh so hard that she shook. As the old woman shook, she turned to stone, and her dark eyes turned back to yellow. Her skin cracked and turned to ash as it fell to the ground. The group stared in amazement at the woman was no longer there. All that remained was a small piece of parchment lying on top of the ashes. It matched the same notes that Thea had found before.

Agatha walked over to the ash and picked up the paper, and read it out loud to the group:

'I have a riddle for you: A group of chains rung tight to protect, but alone protects nothing. And he who wears it protects all. Find the answer, and you will find your precious Lilly Quinn.'

"Let me see that," Thea said, holding out her arm. She took the rough piece of paper from Agatha's hand. She felt a surge of energy run through her body as sparks started to fly from her. Her emerald eyes flashed a shade of violet and rolled back into her head. She lowered her head to her chest and then rolled her head back up and looked right at Agatha.

"Are you alright, Thea?" Robin reached out and placed a hand on Thea's shoulder. Her ears were bleeding, and she had to stare at Thea's lips to see how she responded.

"Uh… yeah. I'm better than alright." Thea looked over her shoulder at Robin and Dean with a smile.

"You know what, dear Aggie?" Thea locked her glance back to Agatha, who was now backing away from where Thea stood.

"I remember EVERYTHING!" she screamed with extreme hatred.

Agatha looked terrified but did not say a word. She took a bottle from her belt and threw it to the ground creating pink smoke that shrouded her from Thea's visibility. Agatha had disappeared into the forest before the smoke had cleared.

Tears filled Thea's eyes as she bent down and picked Fig up. She continued to whisper to her sweet little cat as he nuzzled her face. "I remember everything."

Made in the USA
Columbia, SC
06 August 2021